BETO
& THE
APOCALYPSE

DOUG DALGLISH

BETO
& THE
APOCALYPSE

DOUG DALGLISH

Story Sanctum PUBLISHING

Cover image: Krin Van Tatenhove via Midjourney

Cover design and interior formatting provided by Casselberry Creative Design.

Story Sanctum Publishing
Bloomingdale, IL

ISBN: 979-8-9886653-7-3

Dedicated to the students, faculty, and staff of the Presbyterian Pan American School in Kingsville, Texas. (Although none of these stories and characters are taken from real life, I hope they ring true.)

Table of Contents

Prologue - Scene I, Beto

Beto swung gently in his hammock. It had been another hot night and there was no breeze to help keep him cool. He thought about turning on his bedroom fan, but worried about his electricity rations, which were running low for the month. Even though he was leaving today he didn't want to use all of his rations. He hoped maybe his mom would enjoy using them after he was gone.

His neuro chip informed him it was 6:29 a.m., Monday, August 20, 2035, and 89 degrees Fahrenheit. He did the calculation in his head—that would be 32 degrees Celsius. He checked with his neuro chip—the correct answer was 31 degrees Celsius. Pretty close, he thought. His answer would've been counted wrong on the national standardized test, but it was close enough for him.

He slipped out of his hammock and walked over to his third floor window. His artificial foot clicked against the wooden floor. He kept meaning to replace the padding on the bottom of his foot so that he could walk more quietly.

His window looked out over the street and a long line of clean, new residential apartment buildings. His street looked like countless other modern streets in the city of Waterloo, Texas—a long line of buildings, generously surrounded by young trees and shrubs, ending at a central plaza.

A number of people were already walking to work. The electrobus station was two blocks away. If he were going to school today, he would have to start walking to the station by 6:55 a.m. But he wasn't going to that school ever again, so he had plenty of time.

He grabbed his robe and walked to the bathroom. Click-step, click-step, click-step. His foot was beginning to annoy him. He hung up his robe and touched the shower stall. His two-minute water allocation registered.

He stepped into the shower, being careful that his metal foot didn't slip on the tile. He pushed the 30-second button and cool water rained down. After the initial shock of the cold, it felt great. Once the water stopped, he grabbed the ecosoap and lathered up. He shaved what little facial hair he had, then pushed the 30-second button again to rinse off. As soon as the water stopped, he hit the button again. Thirty seconds later, he was finished.

He dried off, put on his robe, and walked to the kitchen. His mom wasn't up yet, or maybe she was and she was reading in her room. His dad had left for work an hour ago.

He looked in a cabinet and grabbed a breakfast disc and a bowl. He sat the bowl on the kitchen table, crumbled the disc into the bowl, and then topped the crumblings with some dried cranberries from the fruit bowl on the table. The resulting granola-like mixture would keep him going until lunch. His neuro chip recommended he drink 1.5 liters of water with breakfast, so he got up and grabbed a glass, then filled it with water from the tap.

"Good morning, mijo!," his mom said, walking out of her bedroom. "I've got a surprise for you. Your father and I rented an electrocar to take you to your new school today."

"Mom, that's crazy," Beto said. "That's going to cost a lot."

"But it will be much more comfortable and it will be easier to talk on the way," his mom said. "We're not going to see you again until Christmas, so I thought it would be nice to have time to talk."

"Good idea," Beto said. Secretly he was worried about what his mom wanted to talk about on the three hundred mile trip.

Prologue - Scene II, The Lindheimer Academy

The old building stood alone in the center of a vast and flat horizon. It was three stories tall, lacked any decorative features, and showed signs of decay from withstanding decades of sea wind and hurricanes. Justo Contreras stood in the salty, sandy parking lot, looking up the concrete stairway leading to the building's entrance. The smell of decaying seaweed and dead fish filled his nose. The hot sun beat down on his face.

Is this the place for me, for us?

Justo walked up the stairs and tried to open one of the glass doors. It was locked. He looked at himself in the reflection of the glass. Tall and thin. His eye sockets seemed a little dark and sunken. In his black suit, he looked like a very somber man, he thought. An undertaker, perhaps. Maybe a tired businessman.

He walked down the stairs and around the building. As he reached the corner of the building, the sea wind hit him and threw him slightly off balance. Sea gulls hovered over the sand. In the distance, a pelican was gliding over the waves. Justo pressed his hand against the corner of the building, to steady himself against the stiff, salty wind. He looked out to the open water, the great Gulf of Mexico, where his beloved Julia died.

"And so here is where I will build my new world," he said quietly to himself.

He heard a car pull into the parking lot near the front entrance of the building. He turned to see the friar priest and the lawyer step out of the car. Justo walked quickly to greet them.

"Brother James," Justo said as he shook the friar priest's hand, "it's good to see you."

The friar priest was a friendly looking man, a little taller than Justo. The attorney was a very well-dressed woman of middle age.

"Justo!" Brother James smiled. "I'm glad you found the place."

"It's hard to miss. It's the only building for miles," Justo said.

"This is the diocesan attorney, Julie Peterson," Brother James said. "I don't believe you've met."

"Julie?" Justo said thoughtfully. "That was my wife's name. Julia."

The attorney smiled and shook Justo's hand, unsure of how to respond to Justo's reference to his deceased wife. For a moment, her professional demeanor dropped, and she felt like an awkward schoolgirl at a loss for words.

"It's good to finally meet you," she said.

"Is everything in order?" Justo asked.

"Let's go inside and we'll show you," Brother James said.

He led them up the steps, unlocked the doors, and arranged them around a little table in the reception area. The attorney passed around a set of papers for each of them.

"As you know, the land is leased to the county which then has a covenant agreement with the diocese. The county can only transfer that covenant to a not-for-profit agency. Probably due to the remote location of the building, your school is the only organization that has shown any interest in the property."

"This is a challenging location," Brother James said, "but I would hate to see this school disappear. We've spent so much of the church's resources to keep it in repair. I hope a new school under your leadership can benefit from the work we've done."

"And before the church operated the school, it was a military facility?" Justo asked.

"Yes," the attorney said. "It was used as barracks and offices for the Navy when it was built, around 1940. After the Korean War it was empty until the church took it over."

"And why did the school fail?" Justo asked.

"The location was simply too remote," Brother James said. "We never learned how to fill the school, with families so distant. But it sounds like your international school has experience with such things."

"We do. With international students, being far from home is just part of the experience," Justo said. "Are there any other challenges in this location I should know about?"

The attorney shot a knowing look at Brother James.

"There is one," Brother James said. "Maybe Ms. Peterson can explain."

"As I said earlier, no other not-for-profit agency has shown an interest in the property," she said. "However, Cruz Mining Corporation would love to get rid of the school. Having people live on this island makes their mining operation more difficult."

"How does a school make their job more difficult?" Justo asked.

"When people have to drink the water, there is a lot more suspicion of industrial waste. Especially when young people are drinking the water."

"They shouldn't be a problem for you," Brother James said. "Just know that they are not excited to have a school at this location."

Justo nodded and continued to look over the documents the attorney had given him.

"You said that, during all the recent storms, the wǎng luò network remained functional?" Justo asked.

"Yes, we have a sturdy antenna array that connects us to the mainland. It's built to withstand tropical storms. And plenty of bandwidth on the neural network. Enough for all the students and faculty to be connected. The Chinese neuro technology requires a lot of bandwidth, but we've always had enough for the school."

Justo nodded. He stood and walked across the reception area towards the windows that looked out to sea.

"This is the place," he said.

"Do you mind if I ask why you're doing this?" the attorney asked. "Schools are closing down across the nation. As the number of infections rise, parents are keeping their children at home. Why try to start a new school?"

"We may very well be facing the end," Justo said. "But I'd like to face it on my own terms."

Prologue - Scene III, Dr. Celeste Esquivel

Two months later, Justo found himself in a crowded convention center, surrounded by educators enjoying their last few days of freedom before school started again. He searched the ballroom for the one person he had come here to meet. It was evening and everyone had beer or wine. Laughter and loud conversation filled the room. Finally, back near the podium, he saw her. Dr. Celeste Esquivel.

He had just finished listening to her lecture, "Mythology and Propaganda for the New World." She was as brilliant as her books made her seem. She had a charisma that made her a great public speaker. She was passionate about her subject. She didn't come across as arrogant. In her professional work she showed a great desire to collaborate with other scholars. She was just the kind of person Justo was searching for.

Justo pushed his way through the crowd, thinking about the number of infectious diseases spreading in a crowd of this size packed so close together. Although Dr. Esquivel was surrounded by several people who were enthusiastically congratulating her on the speech she had just delivered, Justo interjected himself.

"Dr. Esquivel!" he said. "I've been searching for you."

Celeste looked across her circle of admirers. Justo was visibly different from the crowd of half-inebriated people that surrounded her. He was serious. Focused. Sober.

"If you all will excuse me," she said to the crowd, "I have an appointment."

Justo led her out of the ballroom onto a huge balcony looking out over the city of Waterloo. It was quiet out here, but there were other small groups of people sitting at tables or looking out over the city.

"I hate these events," Celeste said.

"You are a very famous person, Dr. Esquivel," Justo said. "You must speak at events like this all the time."

"Please call me Celeste," she said and then sighed. "I've spoken at a few of these big conferences in the last year or two. But how many lecturers come and go through the years? How many brilliant new theories do people espouse today and then ridicule tomorrow?"

Justo raised his eyebrows. "That's a very cynical perspective. Surely your work will have some lasting meaning? It will no doubt help some students see their lives in a new way?"

"Of course," Celeste said. "You're right, I shouldn't be so self-deprecating. But it helps to keep me from thinking too highly of myself at these events."

"You prefer the quiet life of study?" Justo asked.

"Quietness is hard to find these days," Celeste said.

"Maybe I can be of help to you," Justo said as he smiled.

Prologue - Scene IV, El Campo

Two women sat around a small campfire. One was old and her skin was baked by too many years in the sun. The other was middle-aged and slender, with long, straight black hair, streaked with gray and tied back in a tight braid. The sun was setting as the older one stood and poured water over the flames.

"Don't want to be seen at night," she said. She quenched the fire so expertly that almost no smoke arose from the coals.

"The stars are amazing out here at night," the younger woman said.

The old woman agreed, nodding her head.

"We have a lot of time to watch them," the younger woman said. "The nights are so long it can start to drive you crazy. But then I have to admit that I miss the long, dark nights when I'm back in civilization. It's hard to know where I belong."

"That means our plan is working," the older woman said. "This will be our home someday if we succeed."

The younger woman looked around. The land was flat and extended seemingly forever. Nothing could be seen but grass and scrub and cactus.

"How many people are we talking about?" the younger woman asked. "At the very most, how many?"

"How many are there room for?"

"If we were totally on our own… I just don't know. It takes so much land to support just a few of us. Hundreds of acres. Even then, I think we'd start to deplete the food sources. Things grow very slow out here in the desert."

"We'll need to have a number in mind. This is going to be a reality soon."

"Okay, then, here's another factor to consider," the younger woman said. "If we had no outside help at all, and if we had enough land to supply the resources, what would be the survival rate? How many would survive even three years out here?"

"We'd lose a quarter of them—to infection, to hunger and thirst, to snake bites. And ten years out, not half would be alive."

The younger woman considered this. "One half dead?"

She stirred the wet coals and watched the last few red and glowing spots die away.

"But that means half might live," she said. "Let's keep working. We owe it to the ones who survive to get this right."

The Lindheimer School

07:00   Morning Prayers – Auditorium

07:30   Breakfast – Cafeteria

08:00   Environmental Science – Mr. Stewart, Rm. 101

09:00   Church History – Sr. Elizondo - Auditorium

10:00   World History – Ms. Lin, Rm. 201

11:00   Government – Ms. Cavazos, Rm. 202

12:00   Student Government – Cafeteria

12:30   Lunch – Cafeteria

13:00   English – Dr. Esquivel/Ms. Yarlow, Rm. 203

14:00   Calculus – Ms. Solis, Rm. 303

15:00   Sr. Class Seminar – Dr. Contreras/Ms. Solis, Rm. 303

16:00   Work Assignment – Mr. Silva

18:30   Dinner - Cafeteria

Chapter 1 - Justo Contreras

In which Robert "Beto" Gonzalez meets Director Contreras.

Beto hugged his mom, then waved to his dad who was already in the car. His mom got into the electrocar and they drove away. Beto was left alone in the parking lot of the school, the warm salty wind constantly blowing against him. The nonstop wind was aggravating. Just like being here at this school was aggravating. Being here was a constant reminder that he was a failure. He had failed himself and his family. Instead of being sent to jail, the judge had sent him here.

He had just moved into his room, and had met his weird roommate, Simon. Unlike Beto, Simon was actually happy to be here. Evidently there were no good schools in the little town in Mexico where Simon was from.

Everyone said this was a great school. It was less like a punishment and more like an opportunity, his dad had said. You'll get to meet students and make friends from all over the world, his mom had said. But the fact remained that Beto was here because he had broken the law. And now his family and friends and everything he had ever known were three hundred miles away.

Beto did not want to go inside the school. Instead he stood in the parking lot and looked at his surroundings. There was a big, ugly school building. A boys' dorm on the right. A girls' dorm on the left. And then nothing as far as the eye could see. Sand and grass and ocean stretched seemingly forever. No convenience stores. No coffee shops. He thought about running away, but he would probably die in this blazing sunlight. It was hot out here. And it smelled like rotten fish.

According to his neuro chip, it was thirty-seven degrees Celsius. He had changed the thermometer to metric as instructed in the registration materials of this new school. He had a meeting with the headmaster in ten minutes. And he was beginning to sweat in the heat. It was time to go inside.

The school receptionist was watching him as he walked in the door.

"Are you all settled in your room?" she asked. Her nameplate read "Mrs. Mendoza, Registrar." She was a pleasant looking woman. She acted as if she was accustomed to calming down panicky students.

"Yes, ma'am," Beto said. "I'm ready for my meeting with the headmaster."

"You'll make a better impression if you refer to him as director," Mrs. Mendoza said, emphasizing the Spanish pronunciation. "Director Contreras. He's a very formal man."

"Yes, ma'am," Beto replied as politely as he could. "I'll try to remember that."

"Have a seat and the director will be with you soon," Mrs. Mendoza said.

Beto walked around the reception area. There were a number of awards and framed newspaper articles concerning the school. Or rather, concerning the sister-school that was the sponsor of this new school. There was only one article about this new school, and it merely celebrated the opening of the school a few weeks earlier. However, in the center of the wall was a photo of Director Contreras receiving a state-wide award as educator of the year. It was dated 2034, just last year. Perhaps that is why he is the headmaster of this new school, Beto supposed.

"Mr. Gonzalez?" a voice called from behind him.

Beto turned to see the headmaster addressing him. Director Contreras was shorter than Beto had imagined. In fact, Beto was about his same height. He had a friendly smile, and was dressed in a well-tailored, dark suit. Beto rarely saw adults in this kind of old-style dress. Because of the energy rationing, most adults wore more tropical, loose-fitting clothing.

"Welcome to our school, Mr. Gonzalez," the director said. "I am sure you will find it both challenging and enjoyable."

The director spoke with a distinctly Spanish accent.

"Thank you, director," Beto said. Beto thought he should say something else, like "I'm happy to be here," but he wasn't happy to be here. So, he just shook hands and waited for the director to say something.

"Please come into my office and I will speak with you about your academic record," the director said. "And if you have any questions for me, I will be happy to address them."

Beto followed the director. Instead of walking into one of the academic offices located just off of the reception area, they walked up the stairs. The director moved quickly and Beto had trouble keeping up. After climbing the first set of stairs, Director Contreras paused.

"I'm sorry to be going so slowly," Beto said. "I have an artificial foot. It doesn't negotiate stairs very quickly."

"Ah, yes. I saw that in your records. You lost your foot to an infection?"

"Yes, sir. RB 2722. One of the superbugs that we have no antibiotics for," Beto said. "Someday when I stop growing I hope to invest in a really good foot."

"We're seeing too many students affected by the superbugs. Maybe out here on this island there will be fewer of those terrible new bacterial strains."

Beto nodded in agreement. Director Contreras looked around at the grand hallway of the second floor.

"Most of the faculty members have offices on the ground floor. This floor is where most of the classes are held for underclassmen. Upperclassmen are usually on the third floor. As is my office."

Beto looked down the long, dark hallway with door after door of classrooms. The school had a very old, institutional look to it. High ceilings and wide halls. Dark wood trim, with some ornate carvings. There was a slight smell of mildew. The Director continued up the stairs.

The director's office was the first door at the top of the stairs. With the door open, Beto could see the director's desk. This meant the director could also see every student going up and down this stairway, Beto thought.

They entered the office and it was huge — the size of a classroom. On one side of the room was a large table with wooden chairs around it. There was an ornate silver coffee service on a small table against the wall.

"I've only seen those in movies," Beto said, indicating the coffee service. "It must be an antique."

The director nodded. "It belonged to my wife's grandmother."

"And coffee is so rare these days. I've never actually tasted it."

"Ah! Then that may be a small pleasure you will experience here. We often receive coffee as a gift from our African students. Since the coffee industry in Central America was destroyed, there are few other sources."

"Is it much different from the holly tea we drink for breakfast?" Beto asked.

The director frowned. "Although I admire the Americans for reviving the use of their own native holly for caffeinated beverages, I must say it does not compare in flavor or aroma to coffee. But that is merely my preference."

Beto nodded and turned to see the rest of the huge office. Towards the back of the room was the director's desk, and behind it was a magnificent view of the gulf. Beto was transfixed by the view. He walked to the windows and looked out over the ocean.

"It is quite beautiful, is it not?"

"It's amazing," Beto said. "How far away is the water?"

"A little farther than it looks from up here.From the classroom building there is the little plaza with the fountain and then the basketball courts and then the soccer field. And beyond the soccer field is where the beach begins."

Beto looked out for another moment, trying to tell where the sea met the sky. In the haze of the morning they blended together at the horizon. Finally, he turned around to look for a place to sit when his eye was caught by the sight of a framed picture on the wall next to the director's desk. It was the only object on that wall.

The photo was a black and white portrait of a woman looking not at the camera but off into the distance. Beto's gaze was held by the beauty of the woman — the dark hair and dark eyes, the forlorn expression of her face.

"Director," Beto asked, "who is this?"

"That is a photo of my wife, now deceased."

Deceased? Beto felt a wave of sadness move over him as he looked at the face of the woman, knowing she no longer lived.

"I'm sorry," Beto said, unsure what else to say.

"It is a sad thing to lose the love of one's life," Director Contreras said. "I hope it is a feeling you may be spared. But we all suffer sadness and loss, true?" Beto nodded in agreement.

"Please have a seat," the director said, indicating a comfortable-looking upholstered chair. The director himself sat down on a couch facing the chair. Beto sat.

"And speaking of sadness and loss, I see on your

application that you are coming to our school under less than favorable conditions." The director picked up a manila file from his desk. The file had Beto's name on it.

"Yes, sir," Beto answered. He had prepared himself for this line of questioning. "I made a very serious error in judgment that landed me in legal trouble. Due to my favorable academic record and having never been in trouble before, the judge hearing my case decided to offer me a chance to start fresh in another school. I am currently on parole for two years."

"I am familiar with the circumstances that you describe, having spoken at length with your parents. But why have you chosen this school?"

"The judge felt it would be best for me to leave the city," Beto said. "He felt the police and other authorities might be prejudiced against me. He thought putting as much distance between me and the city of Waterloo was a good idea."

"But why *this* school, Mr. Gonzalez? There are many other schools in many different communities."

"It's a religious school, and my parents thought that might be good for me," Beto said. "And the international aspect of the school seemed interesting to me."

Director Contreras nodded, listening intently to Beto. When Beto failed to say anything more, the director smiled. "Most of the students here feel very fortunate to have been granted a place in this school. It is an exceptional school. We choose our students carefully."

"Then why accept me?" Beto asked. "I'm a convict."

"A convict and an exile," Director Contreras said.

"And a student with very high grades. Your past teachers have described you as creative — sometimes too creative for your own good. Many great people throughout history have gotten into trouble because they had not yet learned to control their intelligence and creativity. I see the potential for greatness in you, Mr. Gonzalez."

"Thank you, sir," Beto said. "But I think my record also shows that I often neglect to do my homework. And I'm tardy to class a lot. I'm maybe not as great a student as you think. I manage to get high grades, but honestly, that's because I find it easy, not because I've worked hard at it. School work just hasn't interested me."

"Not yet, perhaps. But maybe you have not yet been challenged by important subjects and great teachers. Perhaps you have not yet discovered your passion," the director said. "We will challenge you here. I think you will find this school both difficult and worthwhile. But if you find it as boring as your last school, you are welcome to leave. This school is for students who are looking for the true purpose of their lives. It will require all of your heart and soul and mind and strength."

"That's a quote from the Bible?" Beto guessed.

"I am glad you recognize the reference," the director said. "But consider the meaning. Many of the students here know this is their one chance to follow their life's purpose. This is not just a school. This is something much bigger, as far as I am concerned."

"How religious do I need to be to fit in here?" Beto asked.

The director laughed.

"I see religion as an ethical foundation to begin building a life. I'm a man of science with no interest in the supernatural. Our school welcomes students from a wide variety of faith backgrounds, and no faith at all is also an option. Now, our chaplain and our board of directors may disagree. But I am the director of this school."

Beto was impressed by the intensity of the man sitting before him. No one had ever spoken to him like this before.

"Wow," Beto said. "This gives me a lot to think about."

"And you have very little time," the director said, quickly springing from the couch. "You have already missed a whole week of testing and school orientation. And we are now almost late to the school assembly. We must hurry or we'll disappoint Maestra Solis, our lead teacher. And that is one crime for which I will not forgive you."

Chapter 2 - Naomi Solis

In which we meet Maestra Solis and the rest of the faculty.

Director Contreras hurried from his office and down the stairs. Beto followed. On the second floor, the director turned down the great hallway. At the very end of the hallway, the doors of the auditorium were just being closed. The director ran and grabbed one door, then ushered Beto inside. The auditorium was packed with students. At first the room was full of hushed voices whispering to each other, but then a woman on the stage approached the podium and the room fell silent.

The director ushered Beto down the aisle, stopping beside a female teacher.

"Ms. Lin," the director said quietly. "This is your new student, Beto Gonzalez."

Ms. Lin directed Beto to a nearby empty seat. Beto sat down quickly and quietly, feeling as if everyone in the quiet auditorium was staring at him. When he looked up, the woman on the stage was looking at him, slightly annoyed.

Beto froze in place, motionless and silent. Eventually, the woman on the stage removed her gaze from Beto and looked over the rest of the student body.

"Now that we are all here," she said, "let me introduce myself. I am the lead teacher of this school, Maestra Naomi Solis. You may refer to me by my title, Maestra. Welcome to the Lindheimer School. You will see around you students from all over the world."

As she spoke, Beto began to think he would end up liking this woman. She was not tall and not slender, but quite pretty. She spoke with intelligence and kindness.

"Each of us, students and faculty, have chosen to come to this isolated place, this lonely island, because we know the importance of education and none of us are willing to settle for anything less than excellence. Look around this island and you will see that there is very little reason for us to be here, if not for your education. I take your education very seriously and I expect you to do the same."

Beto heard whispering around the auditorium and he realized that some students were quietly translating what Maestra Solis was saying to some of the younger students. He remembered hearing that many of the students here did not speak English when they first arrived. Each student had a neuro chip that would translate for them, but the chips were never as accurate and understandable as a fluent human translator. It seemed to Beto that one student of each language had been chosen to quietly translate as Maestra Solis spoke. Evidently each translation was being fed to the students who needed it.

He noticed when the Spanish translator laughed to herself when Maestra Solis pointed out the lack of anything interesting on the island, a moment later many of the young Spanish speakers also laughed. Beto began to search the open neuro channels and he quickly found the Spanish translation. He scanned a few other channels, hearing other languages he didn't know. But then he found an English channel. A female student was providing a running commentary on Maestra Solis' speech.

"Most of the faculty at the Lindheimer School have come here from our previous campus, and have many years of experience in our system. You will come to know them very well. Sister Virginia Elizondo, Ph.D., is our director of religious instruction."

In the auditorium, a thin woman dressed in black stood up and gave a brief nod and smile to the audience.

"The evil witch gave me a B last year on my final paper," the commentator said. "And now that grade is lowering my GPA when it's a class I don't even need for college. I wish she had stayed at the old school."

Beto noticed a few quiet laughs in the audience.

"Ms. Lin Yu-Ju is the head of our history department…"

The teacher that had helped Beto find a seat stood and bowed to the audience. She looked very young. And very pretty.

"She's okay. But we end up learning world history from a Chinese perspective. In college we'll be like, 'Oh yeah, Queen Elizabeth. Wasn't she during the Ming Dynasty?'"

"Natural Science and Mathematics is led by Dr. Carl Stewart…"

An older man dressed in boots and a bolo tie stood up and waved. He seemed to be unable to stand up completely straight.

"He's awesome. Why isn't he the headmaster of the school? Instead we have the crazy man from a gothic novel, wandering around on the beach at night obsessed with his dead wife."

"Our field laboratory program is headed again by Antonio Reyes. Of course, Antonio is in the field as usual, so he's not here today. But you returning students know him well. And for you new students, you will be learning about the Homerista program soon."

"I cannot wait to start in the Homeristas. No classes. No research papers. This spring is gonna be awesome!"

"Finally, I am the head of the English department and your lead teacher. Since most of you will be working hard on learning English, we will spend a lot of time together."

"If she would spend less time with her students and more time with Director Contreras, maybe the school would be better for all of us. She wouldn't be so lonely and he wouldn't be so depressed. And they might give us a little more time to be kids instead of doing homework all the time."

"I'd also like to address some of the worries you may have due to recent items in the news. It seems that every new disaster in the world, whether it's a flood, a wildfire, an epidemic, always leads to tighter restrictions on things that seem to matter most in your lives. Your water rations are decreased, the hours that electricity is available are decreased, your favorite food becomes unavailable… But this has been going on for years, and I've seen students thrive no matter what the outside world is doing. School is fun and exciting no matter the challenges. So, if you can, forget your worries about the world and enjoy your time here. I've dedicated my life to this work and I know that you students are the most hopeful and resilient of all people."

"That's supposed to reassure us?" the commentator said. "Civilization is collapsing, but don't worry. *School is fun!*"

"And now, I'd like to introduce our new headmaster, Director Justo Contreras. Director Contreras received the state educator of the year award last year and we are very lucky to have him with us as we begin this new school!"

"Notice how she has that little smile whenever she talks about him. She is definitely into him."

Director Contreras jogged up the stairs to the stage and shook Maestra Solis' hand.

"A *handshake*? Here's this *beautiful, single, smart* woman who's *totally* in love with you and you *shake* her hand? The man is hopeless!"

"Thank you, Maestra," the Director said. "The school is lucky to have you as our lead teacher. I know all the upperclassmen who know you are very glad you are here with us to begin this new school. And thank you to all of our staff. Working out here will be an intense experience. We are fifty miles from the nearest grocery store, and many of our teachers are fifty miles from their families — those who are not living on campus. But I promise that we will make this experience worthwhile for both our students and our faculty.

"We are a unique school. The U.S. is a nation still struggling with racial and ethnic identity. But we believe a diverse international community is the best environment for education. How can we care for the planet if we do not know the challenges faced by people all over the planet? We invite students here from all over the world, not just to teach them, but to learn from them."

He walked down the stairs and into the auditorium.

"Oh, no! He's coming down into the room. He's about to get in our faces."

"I have two important announcements to begin the year. First, as many of you know, I was the one who started the field laboratory program five years ago. That program has flourished and this new school will now be its home base. It is my hope that every student in this school will be involved in the program in some way. It is my firm belief that the best way to learn is to get out into the real world and learn in real situations."

"Spending a few weeks with Antonio Reyes is the kind of real-world situation I'm looking forward to. That young man is *gorgeous*!"

"Second, I have some very good news that will come as a surprise to all of you, both faculty and students. We will have a guest lecturer with us this school year who is without a doubt one of the most inspiring minds in education in the world today. She is very excited about our field laboratory program and wants to be a part of it.

"Dr. Celeste Esquivel has done ground-breaking work in how cultural mythology shapes and limits educational possibilities. Another way of saying this is that we are limited in what we can achieve by our beliefs. In the generations before Columbus, Europeans had no reason to think you could go east by traveling west. And even if you could, the distances were too far for ships to travel. But Columbus, as a sailor along the western seas of Europe, kept meeting people who told him rumors and stories of lands to the west. Eventually, he believed these stories enough to risk his life trying to reach those lands. And once he did it, the whole world changed.

"Dr. Esquivel's work centers around creating new possibilities by controlling our social mythology. Our parents believed they had to have electricity twenty-four hours a day to be comfortable. They spent huge amounts of money to keep lights on all night. They heated every building every hour of the day in winter. They cooled every building every hour of the day in summer. These were things they believed they must have, even though *no one in the history of the world had ever needed them before*. As you all know, our mythology has changed. We ask ourselves each day, how little can we use, instead of how much. Dr. Esquivel is coming to help us create a mythology for this school, our own mythology, so that we can do things other schools assume are impossible."

"Well that sounds *totally crazy*. We're all going to be lab rats for Director Contreras' new social experiment. Like I said, I'll be very happy to head out into the wilderness with Antonio while the rest of you have your minds altered."

"Finally, I want to welcome each of you to the new possibilities of this school year. Now get to your classes and work hard."

Chapter 3 - Ms. Lin

In which more is learned about Ms. Lin and what it means to be an American.

Beto's mind was swirling as he searched for his first class. His old life was over and gone due to his legal problems, the outside world was, evidently, falling apart, and he was in a new school in which he knew no one.

He followed the instructions from his neuro chip to Ms. Lin's history class on the second floor. He sat at a two-person table, as he was instructed to do by the 'school organizer program' on the neuro net. A few seconds later, a girl sat next to him.

"Hi, I'm Adriana," the girl said.

"Hi, Adriana. I'm Beto."

"You're new."

"I am."

"This is a really good school," Adriana said. "You'll like it. Everyone is very friendly here."

Beto noticed that Adriana spoke with a heavy Spanish accent. She had a cute, round face, long, brown, wavy hair and brown eyes. All in all, she was kind of average looking. Except there was something odd about her right eye.

"You went to the old school?" Beto said. "What was it like?"

"Much the same as this one. This school is in a more isolated place. But the ocean is beautiful. I really like it here."

"All these teachers came from the old school?" Beto asked.

"Yes, we know most of them well. They are very dedicated to teaching here at a very small school. The teachers are great. They really care about us."

"Awesome," Beto said, wondering if everyone was so enthusiastic about the school. *Either this girl is brainwashed, or this place is like a little paradise.*

"Hey!" someone behind Beto said. "You're an American."

Beto turned around and saw two boys. One smiling at him and one looking very serious, almost depressed.

"You know how I can tell you're an American?" the smiling boy said.

Beto shrugged, not sure if this was the beginning of some kind of hazing or something.

"You have the NC3 neuro chip," the boy said, pointing to the chip behind his own ear. "Those of us on student visas can only have the NC2. We can't get video. And we can only access the short version of Wiki Mem."

"Really?" Beto said. "I didn't know that."

"By the way, my name is Gonzalo," the boy said.

"Good to meet you. I'm Beto."

"Did you notice how Adriana's right eye kind of moves slower than her left?" the boy asked. "She has an artificial eye. The NC2 chip makes it move just a little too slow to look natural."

Beto looked at Adriana, who didn't look embarrassed at all.

"Wow. I didn't notice your eye," he lied. "It looks great…very natural."

"Thank you," Adriana said, smiling.

"But with a chip like yours, her eye would be perfect. The NC3 is awesome," Gonzalo continued. "Yeah, Juan and I are going to make sure we study with you," the boy said, pointing to himself and then the silent boy next to him.

Ms. Lin walked in and the class started to turn their attention to her. Ms. Lin was small in stature and relatively young, but she held herself with a degree of authority. She gave a stern glance at Gonzalo and he immediately stopped talking.

Adriana leaned close to Beto and whispered, "You'll like those two. Juan is really smart. And Gonzalo is very friendly."

"Thanks," Beto whispered back.

Ms. Lin began to write something on the board in Chinese.

"She does this every year," Adriana whispered to Beto.

Beto watched closely as she wrote. Ms. Lin had short black hair and wore a short-sleeved, high-collared white dress. She actually looked a little too formal for school. Beto usually didn't pay much attention to fashion, however, Ms. Lin's prim appearance inspired him to brush the dust off his khaki pants and straighten his simple, cotton, button-up school shirt.

After the first two symbols, Ms. Lin began writing in English, "It is not the failure of others to appreciate your abilities that should trouble you, but rather your failure to appreciate theirs. (Analects 1.16)"

Adriana wrote this in her spiral notebook, so Beto did the same. He wasn't accustomed to physically writing notes, he usually just made mental notes on his NC3 chip, but Adriana seemed like a good student and Beto was going to try to be a better student than he had been in the past.

"Every week I will write a quote from Master Kong on the board. You may also know him by the name of Confucius. These first two symbols say, "The master said," Ms. Lin explained. "The quote will be part of the ongoing theme we will be discussing each week as we move through world history. Now, I want you to get in groups of four, learn each other's names, and where each person is from. Then discuss what this saying means to you in the culture in which you were raised. You have five minutes."

Gonzalo quickly moved his chair next to Beto's table. He kissed Adriana on the cheek. Juan slowly brought his chair over.

"Gonzalo. Juan. Adriana. All from Mexico," Gonzalo said. "Where are you from, Beto?"

"Wait," Adriana said. "I think Ms. Lin expects a little more detail than that. I'm Adriana Cavazos Aguilar.

I'm from a city called Xalapa in the state of Veracruz. And as Gonzalo has already pointed out, I lost one eye due to an infection three years ago. But my electronic eye is very good, so I guess I am lucky I can still see."

Beto started writing this down. "Adriana Aguilar. From... how do you spell the city you're from?"

"No," Gonzalo said. "Her last name is Cavazos. Our first last name is our last name in America. Our second last name in Mexico is something you don't even have in America."

"You have two last names?" Beto asked. "And the first one is the one I need to know?"

"Si," Gonzalo replied. "And the city is X-A-L-A-P-A. Like jalapeno, but with an 'x.'" Because that is where jalapenos come from."

"*Really?*" Beto laughed, not sure whether this was a joke or not.

"*Really,*" Adriana said. She looked sincere and so Beto assumed she was.

"Well, I'm Roberto Gonzales from Waterloo, Texas. People call me Beto."

Adriana started writing this down. Then she looked at Gonzalo.

"Gonzalo Huerta Narciso, from Matamoros, Tamaulipas, Mexico. I have two normal eyes."

Beto laughed politely, but looked to make sure Adriana wasn't offended. She looked okay. Then, everyone looked at Juan and awaited his reply.

"Juan Guzman Mendoza, also from Matamoros. I have the NC2 chip like Gonzalo, but I haven't filled mine up with games, so it works pretty fast. Not as fast as yours, though."

Suddenly, Beto's neuro chip signaled an emergency. The room fell silent. Evidently everyone had received the same warning.

"Everyone please stay seated and remain calm. The headmaster has issued a campus security alert," Ms. Lin said.

The class sat quietly. A group of girls near the door whispered and giggled. One of them caught Beto's attention. She was absolutely gorgeous.

"Who is that girl over there, talking?" Beto quietly asked Adriana.

"The loud one?" Adriana said. "That's Marisa. The Voice, as we call her. She's the one who has her own channel on the neuro chip network."

"Is she the one who was commenting on all the teachers this morning during Maestra Solis' assembly?"

"That's her. She has a very sharp tongue," Adriana said.

"Doesn't she get in trouble for that?" Beto asked.

"The faculty doesn't have time to worry about everything each student says," Adriana explained. "Especially that one. No one would ever get anything done if they had to monitor her."

Beto looked up and noticed that the entire class was staring at him and Adriana. They had drifted closer together during their whispered conversation, and now they were almost head to head. Ms. Lin was also staring at them.

"If you are finished, Adriana," Ms. Lin said, "The

headmaster has an announcement. A student who, for some reason, was not in class this morning has been injured. He was wandering near the old soccer field and was bitten by a snake."

Ms. Lin put her hands on her hips and turned her attention from her neuro chip to the class.

"You all know that that area is off-limits. We caught dozens of snakes out there before we finally condemned the area."

Beto heard the sound of a helicopter. Several students rushed to the window to see the medivac chopper land on the soccer field.

"Hey, that's Simon!" someone said.

Beto ran to the window. His roommate was being carried onto the helicopter.

"Please have a seat, class," Ms. Lin said. "Whatever Simon was doing out there during class time is none of our business right now. He is being cared for. Now, let's come back to order."

She looked around the room. She made eye contact with Beto and then looked down at her students' roll.

"Beto," she said. "You are new to our school. Why don't you tell us where you are from and what this saying from Master Kong means to you."

Beto froze. He wasn't great at public speaking, especially not when he had to be the first one to speak in front of new people. As he stood up, he looked around at all the faces staring at him. Marisa looked like she was about to laugh out loud at his obviously nervous behavior. And then he looked down at Adriana. She was giving him an encouraging look and that helped him to calm down a little. He took a deep breath.

"My name is Beto Gonzalez and I'm from Waterloo, Texas," he said.

"Would you mind pointing that out on the world map?" Ms. Lin said.

Beto walked over to the giant map on the wall.

"Here we are on the south coast of Texas, on the barrier island," he said. "I am from the central part of Texas, near the hill country. About three hundred miles away. Waterloo is the state's new capital."

"Interesting," Ms. Lin said. "Many of our students from Mexico are closer to home than you are."

Beto nodded and felt a little depressed about this observation. Home was a long way away.

Marisa raised her hand.

"Can you tell us why the state has a new capital?" she asked.

Beo noticed that Marisa spoke English very well. She must be a U.S. native. And therefore, she probably already knew why Texas' capital was moved.

"The capital used to be called Austin, after one of the early English-speaking colonists in the area," Beto said. "But after a series of conservative governors let the state grow more and more polluted, while they simultaneously reduced state funding of public health to almost nothing, a fungal infestation spread throughout the buildings of the city. Eventually, too many buildings were uninhabitable. Hundreds of buildings were torn down, but the fungus continued to live in the soil. The core of the city had to be abandoned, and slowly even the suburbs emptied out. No one wanted to risk their life by staying in the area. And so, a new, cleaner capital was built a safe distance away. A lot of cities have seen similar circumstances, but Austin was a particularly bad case."

Many of the students cringed as they listened to this story. Beto assumed they had friends or family members who were victims of deadly fungal infections.

"And now for the saying," Ms. Lin said. "What would that mean to people in Waterloo, Texas?"

Beto lifted up his spiral and read the saying again. He actually had no idea what it meant. His neuro chip was feeding him a list of articles about Confucius, but nothing seemed to relate to this particular saying. So much of his brain was nervous about being watched by the entire class that he had very little brain power left to try to untangle Chinese wisdom.

Adriana spoke up, "I was part of Beto's group and I think we were talking about teamwork, about how it is good to study with others because then we can benefit from each person's abilities."

Ms. Lin was willing to accept that answer and move on to get input from another group. Beto collapsed back into his chair, relieved that the ordeal was over.

"Thanks," he whispered to Adriana.

Adriana smiled back. Beto heard very little of the rest of the class discussion. But he did have the presence of mind to write down his homework assignment in his spiral. When the bell rang, Gonzalo grabbed Beto and Adriana and led them to the dining hall. Juan tagged along silently.

Chapter 4 - The Homeristas

In which Juan reveals a few of his many interests and the homeristas are introduced to the student body.

They went through the lunch line as a group and found a table where they could sit together.

"I noticed you were doing a lot of note-taking in Ms. Lin's class," Gonzalo said. "I'll bet everything you need to know about the class is accessible through your NC3 chip. Ms. Lin writes stuff out for the rest of us who can't download all of her notes."

"I was just doing what Adriana was doing," Beto said.

Adriana smiled. "I think you are wise to write everything down, Beto. I think it helps you to remember. And you learn things in a different way when you write it down."

"I'm just saying that if I had that chip I could do a lot less work and learn a lot more," Gonzalo said.

Beto felt a little awkward having access to better technology than the rest of the students. He looked down at his lunch. It was salad, a vegetable, a breaded patty of some kind, and a wheat roll.

"I love this NutriVitaPro," Gonzalo observed as he cut up his patty and ate enthusiastically.

Beto thought it tasted like any other school food. It tasted a lot better with ketchup.

"NutraVitaPro was developed for college athletes," Juan said, matter-of-factly. This was the first time Beto remembered Juan speaking.

"Really?" Beto said.

"It has a complete vitamin and mineral complex, plus the highest quality animal and vegetable proteins," Juan said.

"Juan knows a lot about NutraVitaPro," Gonzalo said.

"I thought this was just a soy burger," Beto said.

"No, in fact, the recipes for NutriVitaPro differ depending on the region of the world that it's made in, but they avoid using soy," Juan continued. "Unfermented soy has compounds similar to female hormones, which wouldn't be good for athletes in training."

Beto nodded. Adriana was politely paying attention, but Beto thought she looked as if she had heard all this many times before.

"Well, I think I'll enjoy it a lot more now that I know how good it is for me," Beto said. It tasted a lot like cardboard and stale peas.

"They have a clever marketing scheme," Juan said. "They originally developed it for college athletes in the U.S. and they gave it away for free to some of the nation's best teams. It gave them such good results in terms of fitness and performance that other college programs wanted to buy it. But they only sold it to a few programs at first, and so there was a lot of excitement about who would get it and when."

"We still can't get it in Mexico," Gonzalo said. "The national university has it, but no one else."

"And so we are lucky to have it here," Juan said.

This was something else Beto had taken for granted that his new classmates thought was unique and special. He was beginning to realize how easy it would be for him to seem like a spoiled rich kid to the other students.

"Juan is a very serious soccer player," Adriana said. "Do you play any sports, Beto?"

"No," Beto said. "I lost my right foot to an infection a few years ago. I have an artificial foot that isn't very good for sports."

"Really?" Juan said with a little too much enthusiasm. "Let me see!"

"Juan, that's rude!" Adriana exclaimed.

"No, it's okay," Beto said, as he lifted up his foot onto his chair and rolled up his jeans. He pulled off his shoe and lowered his sock to reveal that his foot was made of plastic and steel. "The infection started in one of my toes and started to infect the whole foot. They say I was lucky they were able to remove all the infection and save my leg."

"I'm so sorry," Adriana said.

"It's okay. I'm used to it now," Beto said.

"So you can't play soccer?" Juan asked.

"Kicking is really painful."

"What about running?" Juan asked.

"I can jog slowly, but I think I look funny doing it. I'm kind of awkward."

Juan kept staring at Beto's foot. After a while, it began to feel awkward.

"You'll have to excuse Juan," Adriana says. "He tends to get obsessed about some things. He's probably designing a new foot for you in his head."

"No, I agree, it is kind of interesting," Beto said. "I've done a lot of reading on different types of prostheses. Someday I may have a few different types to try out for different things — one for running, one for mountain climbing... who knows?"

"By the way, Juan, I noticed you were taking lots of notes in Ms. Lin's class," Adriana said. "But you were writing a lot more than she was saying."

"A drone flew by. Probably from the naval air station in Corpus Christi, checking out the helicopter that flew in," Juan answered.

"Juan has an impressive list of drone sightings," Gonzalo said. "He's working on a theory of what they are up to and what they might be watching."

"Drones?" Beto said.

"Unmanned aircraft," Juan said. "They show up whenever there's anything happening on campus. When students first arrive, they're here a lot. The strange thing is, they can observe things from miles away and remain unseen. When we see them here it's because someone wants them to be seen."

The bell rang. Beto's neuro chip told him it was time for another assembly. But this time it was not in the auditorium, it was outside on the plaza.

"It's time for the homeristas!" Gonzalo said. "You'll enjoy this!"

They hurried outside and Gonzalo pushed Beto to the front of the crowd gathering around the courtyard. Adriana and Juan followed. Director Contreras was there, as was Maestra Solis and most of the other teachers.

"Who is that pretty woman next to the director?" Adriana asked.

Gonzalo touched his neuro chip. "That's what the Voice is talking about right now. Someone found a photo of Dr. Esquivel online and that seems to be her."

"Wow!" Adriana said. "She is gorgeous. Maestra Solis is going to have a hard time competing with that."

Beto silently agreed. Dr. Esquivel was hard to describe. She was tall and had long, dark hair that was blowing in the sea breeze. She was dressed in a tailored suit. Her face was slender and beautiful. She was, in a word, perfect.

Beto tuned in to the Voice.

"I just don't like her. She's too perfect. I mean, look at Maestra Solis. She's pretty, but she's humble. She wears glasses — fashionable glasses. She dresses nice, but she's not showing off. This new woman is just too much. I don't trust her."

Then the Voice and the crowd fell quiet. Out on the flat, grassy plain, a group of people were walking towards the plaza. They looked rugged. They looked strong. They all wore high leather boots, Beto noticed, presumably as protection from snakes. The man walking in the lead was dark and built like an athlete. He walked like Beto wished he could walk, with confidence and perfect grace.

"Here he comes!" the Voice said. "Now, those guys look impressive. I wonder what the city girl Dr. Esquivel thinks about this?"

The leader looked like a character out of some 19th-century adventure novel. He had dark skin, longish hair, and wore a loose, white cotton shirt — long-sleeved but with the sleeves rolled up. He had a wide-brimmed hat. Around his neck was a necklace made up of seashells. At his waist was a long knife. Over his shoulder he carried a primitive-looking bow and a quiver of arrows.

The young woman walking at his side looked African. She was dressed similarly to the man but wore no hat. And she walked with a very tall walking stick.

A half dozen young people followed behind. They looked wild and serious, and they were all armed with bows and knives.

"Who are they?" Beto asked Adriana.

"Los homeristas," Adriana said. "The field laboratory group."

"When I heard field laboratory, I was thinking of scientists in lab coats," Beto said.

"They live in the wild," Adriana said. "And they do all kinds of experiments as if they had no contact with the modern world. We don't see them for months at a time."

"Wow! That sounds intense," Beto said.

Director Contreras took a step up onto the concrete seating area that surrounded the fountain. The crowd stopped murmuring. The homeristas stood just outside the plaza area in the tall grass, as if they were hesitant to walk on a sidewalk.

"Okay, guys, the Voice is signing off for a while. I want to see what is about to happen and I don't have time to explain it all to you." The Voice channel fell silent.

"For those of you who are new to our school, let me introduce our field laboratory program. For the people who lived in this land before the coming of Europeans, the land provided everything they needed. Their food, their clothing, their medicines, all their technology came from the land and the sea that surrounds us. With our modern eyes, we look out at this landscape and it seems empty. All of our food and clothing and medicine and technology come from far away and we may know nothing of how it is made or even what materials it is made of. But for the native mind, this land is full of gifts and wonders.

"The field laboratory program is designed to help us learn once again to appreciate both the wonders of the natural world and the wonders of our human ability to live as an integral part of the native ecosystem. Although these students," he gestured to the group standing outside the plaza, "look wild and maybe even savage, they are collecting volumes of scientific data each semester. How do they survive the cold in the winter? How do they find enough water in a summer drought? When they dig up roots to eat for survival, how long does it take for that same number of roots to grow again? When you join the field laboratory project, you will be investigating questions like this.

"Does this sound a little academic?" the director

asked rhetorically. He looked down to Mr. Stewart, and Mr. Stewart threw him an apple. The director caught it and continued to speak. "Food this sweet and beautiful is hard to find in the natural world. This amount of nutrition and water would be a treasure in the south Texas summer. But imagine this was a bird or a small animal. It is nutritious, but it is fast. How do you bring it home for dinner?"

The director tossed the apple high into the air, in a tall arc away from the students. The leader of the homeristas, smoothly and quickly slipped the bow from his shoulder, notched a small arrow on the string, and sent the arrow flying through the apple as it fell to the ground.

The crowd of students and teachers applauded enthusiastically. Beto noticed that Dr. Esquivel was also impressed.

"Thank you, Antonio," the director said, as he also applauded. "To let such a treasure of food get away could mean death in the wilderness. Antonio has worked in this program for five years. He knows how to survive. But what of the younger students? Each of these students was just like you one year ago. After one year, are they able to survive?"

The director looked down to Mr. Stewart again. Mr. Stewart threw him another apple. And then another. And then another. The Director held up three apples. Three of the younger homeristas prepared their bows and notched their arrows.

"Let's find out," the Director said as he tossed all three apples into the air. Three arrows flew. Two found their mark.

"Not everyone survives," the Director said. He

jumped down off the bench and walked over to the undamaged apple. He picked it up and examined it, then held it up.

"The arrow cut through one side relatively deeply," he said. "Maybe all of the students would have survived today."

The crowd applauded again. The director jumped back onto the bench.

"For the rest of today, the homeristas will be here to answer your questions," he said. "All juniors and seniors with passing grades are eligible to join the year-long program. If you do not feel like an entire year in the outdoors is what you want to do, you may apply to take part in a shorter project. There is a list of projects on the class syllabus. Sophomores and freshmen may apply to the program but, due to a need to limit class size, very few of you will be admitted this year. The best way to be admitted if you are an underclassman is to submit an impressive project proposal. If your proposal is chosen, you will be welcomed into the program."

Antonio stepped forward.

"If you're ready to turn off your neuro chips for a while and live in the real world, this is your opportunity," he said.

The crowd began to burst with animated conversations as the director jumped down from the bench. He and Dr. Esquivel walked off with Antonio and another homerista. The rest of the student body swarmed around the remaining homeristas, welcoming them home and asking them questions.

Chapter 5 - Homero Lopez

In which stories are told around the campfire, including the story of Homero Lopez and the explanation for Dr. Esquivel's presence.

The rest of the afternoon was filled with demonstrations of how to find edible plants, games that could be played with easy-to-find natural objects, and many other topics that fascinated Beto. Dinner was cooked over open fires on the beach. After the sun sank below the horizon, Beto found himself sitting on the sand next to Adriana and Gonzalo. His head was spinning from the things he had seen and learned.

"Adriana, you were right," Beto said. "This school is amazing."

"I told you so," Adriana said. She looked out to sea as the wind played with her long hair. Beto wondered about the kiss between Gonzalo and Adriana from earlier in the day. It was a clear sign of affection, but he hadn't seen any other indication that Gonzalo and Adriana were anything other than good friends.

"You like the field laboratory project?" Gonzalo said.

"It is amazing! Are we interested in it?" Beto asked.

Gonzalo looked at Adriana. Adriana nodded.

"It kind of scares me, but I think I would like to do it next year when I'm a junior," she said.

"Juan and I are hoping to get in this year," Gonzalo said. "You haven't seen Juan today because he's working on his project proposal."

"This year?" Beto asked. "When would you leave?"

"When do *we* leave, you mean? You're coming with us," Gonzalo said.

"A year in the wilderness?" Beto said incredulously. "I don't think I'm ready for that. Was Antonio serious about having no neuro chips?"

"No one is ever ready for it," Gonzalo said. "And I've heard students get to use their neuro chips most of the time. We'll need them for the scientific parts, right? But think about it. This is a once-in-a-lifetime chance. If we get in this year, that would mean we could be in the program for three years. We would be like Antonio! Think about how much that would change your life."

Beto looked at Adriana.

"Don't look to me for an answer," she said. "I'm not going to talk you out of it. If you three make it in this year, then you can take care of me when I enter the program next year."

Beto felt a thrill run up his spine. He had been expecting to be bored in a small private school. Now he was as scared as he had ever been in his entire life by this unexpected opportunity.

They heard footsteps running across the sand. It was

Juan.

"Hey, guys!" he said as he tried to catch his breath. "Grace Nkuzi is getting ready to tell a story by the campfire."

Adriana and Gonzalo jumped up to follow Juan, who was already running to the campfire. Beto followed. When they arrived, a small group had already gathered. Front and center near the fire was Dr. Esquivel with Antonio. Dr. Esquivel had changed into a light cotton dress and leather chanclas. She still looked amazing.

Beto looked for a place to sit. He hesitated to sit next to Adriana again, in case Gonzalo might want to be with her. But Gonzalo was talking with Juan and they found a place to sit on their own. Beto quickly sat next to Adriana before anyone else could. Adriana gave him a very warm and welcoming smile.

"Grace has been in los homeristas for two years," Adriana said. "She's from Rwanda."

Grace was a small person, slender, but strong. She was dressed in a very simple sundress. She wore what looked like hand-made sandals. Her hair was cut short to the scalp. She sat on a log of driftwood facing the fire across from Beto.

"I've been asked to tell the story of Homero Lopez, the man for whom we homeristas are named," Grace said.

The circle of people around the fire fell silent.

"Homero Lopez came to the United States as a simple manual laborer. He worked hard and sent money home to his family, but he grew dissatisfied with his life. He decided to return to his home in Nuevo Laredo, beginning his trip from the city of Corpus Christi. Since he was an undocumented worker, he planned to travel home by secret means, as many people do, avoiding highways where he could be arrested and detained. It was early in November when he messaged his wife to say he was returning home.

"The trip was a long and dangerous one, his wife knew. She did not know when to expect him home, but by the end of December she began to worry. Many weeks passed and she had no word from him. After several months, she assumed the worst—that he had died or been killed in the deserts of south Texas.

"Two years passed and she heard nothing. Then one day, a man arrived in her neighborhood who had just returned from the United States. He was drinking in a bar and telling stories when someone heard him mention Homero's name. The people of the town brought the man to Homero's wife, and he told her everything he knew, which was not much. He had been trying to cross a particularly deserted and wild region when he ran low on food and water. Just when he was resigned to the fact that he might die, a man found him and gave him aid. The man was Homero Lopez, and he was living in a cave by an old, dry river. The traveler described Homero as living quite comfortably. He had plenty of food from wild plants and an occasional animal he managed to trap. He dressed in coyote skins, for it was winter. And the cave in which he lived was decorated with beautiful paintings.

"The traveler asked Homero about the paintings, which were of wild animals and creatures that looked like angels and demons and giant men. Homero said that these were creatures he had met on his journey. The giants were inhabitants of forbidden regions of the desert. The angels were beings who had helped him learn to survive. The demons he would not speak of, but he said the traveler would know them if he ever met them.

"The traveler spent several days with Homero and watched him weave fibers from desert plants into rope and baskets and sandals. He watched him crush dried plants to make dyes for his artwork. Homero collected and dried foods to save for times when there would be no food to gather. He had dug out cisterns in the cave to hold water for times of drought. And he had many, many stories to tell of his adventures—stories of ghosts and strange creatures the traveler had never heard of before.

"When the traveler asked Homero why he stayed in the desert rather than go home, Homero said that he was waiting for something or somebody. There was a guest he was expecting. During a violent thunderstorm, a strange and intelligent creature had taken shelter with him in his cave. The creature said it would return to thank Homero, and that was what he was waiting for. But he would say nothing more of the visitation.

"Finally the traveler decided it was time for him to continue his journey. Homero gave him food and what little water he could carry in dried gourds, then pointed him in the right direction. He reminded the traveler of the names of his wife and two sons and asked that the traveler tell his family he was still alive. The traveler walked for four days before he found a highway. And then he eventually found Homero's family.

"After this amazing news, Homero's wife continued

to wait for him. After two more years, she began to despair that he would never come home. Finally, in the fifth year of his journey Homero walked into his home neighborhood and the neighbors celebrated and accompanied him to his home and his wife. Homero hugged his wife and his two sons and said he was glad to be home. He was dressed in regular clothing, with no animal skins or woven sandals. He announced that he was going to begin work as an auto mechanic, a trade he had never practiced before. And when people asked him about the stories the traveler told about him, he acted as if he had no idea what they were talking about. He resumed his life and never spoke publicly of his five-year journey. However, the neighbors say that Homero and his wife sometimes entertain strange visitors—people who arrive at night and leave before dawn."

Grace ended the story.

"And that is why we call our field lab students las homeristas?" a student asked.

"In honor of his five year journey and of the wonders he experienced during that time," Grace answered.

"But do the strange creatures, the ghosts and demons, really exist?" another student asked. Antonio sat up and spoke. "Since our purpose is scientific exploration, we report only what we have seen and documented," he said. "However, there are some intense experiences we have survived — storms and floods and endless days of sun and heat. I can imagine a man alone out there might have some very real experiences that he would later describe as magical."

"So you have never seen a demon yourself?" Dr.

Esquivel asked.

Antonio laughed.

"There are some scary and dangerous people traveling through those lands," he said. "They are very real, very human people, but we deal with them pretty much the way we would deal with demons. And some of the landowners we work with have been angels to us."

"Hmm," Dr. Esquivel smiled as she considered Antonio's answer. "What do you see as the major goal of the homerista project? Antonio? Grace?"

Grace answered first. "I just want to learn more about the natural world and how people fit into it. It is a beautiful thing to be out there. Maybe my goal is just to have the privilege of being out there."

Dr. Esquivel nodded in appreciation of Grace's answer. "Antonio?" she said.

"The goal is to rediscover a better way of relating to our land. We hope to develop and spread a broad range of practices for the conservation and use of the land around us. From eating native foods in a sustainable way, to encouraging more biodiversity on our managed lands... even just spending more time with the land in a non-destructive way."

"That sounds like a wonderful and worthy goal," Dr. Esquivel said.

"But tell us, what is your goal in being here?" Antonio asked. "Why has Director Contreras invited you here?"

Dr. Esquivel smiled brightly. She took a moment to think.

"Your director knows that he is very comfortable and competent working with science and technology," Dr. Esquivel said. "But people need more than that when they are deciding how they will live their lives. We are not very logical people. We live by beliefs and stories of who we are and who we strive to be. I study stories and how they affect people. Your director has invited me to help this school write its own story, to create its own mythology."

"How can you, as an outsider, help us write our own story?" Antonio asked.

"You are right to be suspicious of outsiders interpreting your story," Dr. Equivel said. "But my goal is to listen and to collect your stories. I want to listen to the emotions and aspirations I hear when the students speak about their experiences. Then, as an outsider, I can tell you what I am hearing and help you to distill all the stories down into some very important themes. But that is only what I hear. You have to take the next step of finding ways to help those themes to grow as you tell your own stories to future students."

"How long will you be here?" Grace asked.

"Director Contreras has asked me to commit to working with all of you for this school year. If we all like the progress we are making, I could be working with you for much longer."

Gonzalo suddenly appeared next to Beto and sat down. He handed Beto a note.

"Juan gave me this note," Gonzalo said. "He has confirmed that Marisa is definitely applying to the homeristas this semester."

"What does that have to do with us?" Beto asked.

"Are you kidding me? I want to spend a whole school year with Marisa in the wild. That sounds like heaven to me," Gonzalo said.

Beto stood up and pulled Gonzalo to his feet. He dragged Gonzalo away from the fire.

"You're interested in *Marisa*? What about *Adriana*?" Beto asked.

"*Adriana*?" Gonzalo looked confused. "She's my friend, but I don't think of her like that."

"But I saw you kiss her this morning in class," Beto said.

Gonzalo laughed. "We're from Mexico. We kiss everyone. But seriously, Adriana and I are very good friends but that's all. Marisa is the girl for me."

"But every guy in the school wants to be with her, from what I've seen," Beto said. "Why would she choose you? No offense, but there's a lot of guys here."

"She'll choose me because I am the most romantic," Gonzalo said. "Plus she has to choose someone, right? And most guys are too intimidated by her. But not me. I will win her over. But tell me, what about you and Adriana?"

"Adriana? I just met her today," Beto said.

"But do you like her?" Gonzalo asked.

"Of course, she's great," Beto said.

"And she's given you all of her time today," Gonzalo said. "I think she likes you."

"I plan to just see how it goes," Beto said. "I think these things have to happen naturally."

Gonzalo pointed back to the fire, where a senior

boy, a homerista, had just sat down next to Adriana and was talking to her.

"I think something is happening naturally right now," Gonzalo said. "Don't wait too long."

Beto looked at Adriana and the boy and he definitely felt a twinge of jealousy. *But just a few minutes ago I was thinking of Adriana just as a friend*, he thought. *And I was in the club of guys falling for Marisa*. Beto felt torn. Marisa seemed more and more out of his reach, and Adriana was right in front of him. He carefully weighed the options, then walked with purpose back towards Adriana. He managed to stay by her side the entire evening.

They all went back to their dorms long after lights-out. Beto was exhausted from a long day filled with new experiences. He was about to fall asleep when there was a knock on his window. It was Gonzalo.

"Quickly!" Gonzalo said. "Marisa's set up an encrypted channel for a student discussion tonight. The encryption formula won't work on my NC2 chip."

"What do you want me to do?" Beto asked.

"Your encryption key is the student number found on your registration documents. There's an invitation to tonight's secret meeting on the neuro net."

"What keeps teachers from listening in?" Beto asked. "Entering our student registration number seems pretty obvious."

"It's after midnight," Gonzalo said. "What kind of adult is going to put that much effort into secretly monitoring us?"

Beto found the invitation using his NC3 chip and mentally entered his number.

"Beto is joining us," the Voice said.

"Link me in," Gonzalo said.

"Is that Gonzalo I hear?"

"Your encryption is keeping most of us out," Gonzalo said loud enough to be heard through the vibrations in Beto's ears, which then stimulated the neural connection.

"Shoot!" Marisa said. "Sometimes I get carried away. That explains why there's so few of us tonight."

"Just turn off the encryption and we can all join," Gonzalo said.

"The topic is sensitive," Marisa said. There was a pause. "But it will be a boring conversation with all U. S. kids. You're right, I'll just stop the encryption."

A moment later, Gonzalo was able to join in the conversation. Several others joined in as well.

"Tonight, we're discussing theories of the director's true plan for the school," Marisa said. "The crazier, the better."

"It's gotta be a cult," Kim, a student from Korea, said. "And that would explain why Dr. Esquivel is here. She'll help brainwash us to do whatever the director's ultimate plan is."

"How do we protect ourselves from brainwashing?" Gonzalo asked.

"If she's good at her job, there's nothing we can do," Kim said. "We're destined to serve the director's dark purposes."

"What if the director is planning some kind of

revolution?" someone asked.

"We're training with bows and arrows," Marisa said. "The U. S. military would crush us in a matter of minutes."

"True."

"Could he be a Dr. Frankenstein, using students to create a new zombie wife?"

"That's a good one," Marisa said. "We'll have to be on the look out for missing students."

"Or students missing body parts," Beto added. "There's a lot of us missing appendages. Who's keeping track?"

"What about a plan to take this part of Texas back into Mexico?" Gabriela asked. Gabriela was known for her love of Mexican history. "When Texas left Mexico, the southern border was still in dispute. This new school lies in the disputed territory."

"Interesting. But wasn't that dispute settled more than a hundred years ago?" Marisa asked.

"Some of us have long memories," Gabriela said. "And we hold grudges."

"We're on the coast," Beto said. "He could be smuggling something."

"Smuggling what?" Marisa said.

"I don't know. What do people smuggle?" Beto said. "Drugs. People."

"Or what if he's not bringing stuff in, but smuggling it out?" Gonzalo said. "Like NC3 chips. We could use those in Mexico."

The ideas grew wilder and wilder until they were all getting too tired to continue.

"Of course, no one has mentioned the scariest possibility," Marisa said. "What if we're spending four years, sitting through classes, in order to earn the right to go to college and sit through another four years of classes, in order to earn the right to sit in a cubicle for twenty years working for a big corporation."

"Terrifying!" Kim said. "I think I'd choose being a zombie bride over that."

Marisa ended the session around 2 a. m.

"Good job, everyone! Great ideas! I think we're a little closer to understanding why we've been sent to this god-forsaken island. Stay alert. And keep us informed of any new developments," she said.

The channel fell silent. Gonzalo snuck back to his room and Beto fell asleep with the sound of the surf and the smell of the salt air. *I'm liking this god-forsaken island.*

Chapter 6 - Seafood and the Uranium Mine

In which Mr. Stewart teaches about sea life and Ms. Yarlow warns of uranium contamination.

Beto sat in the chapel for morning prayers. The chapel was tall, almost three stories tall, and dark. The sun was not yet shining through the geometric stained glass windows. Two candles were lit on the simple wooden table at the front. There were no paintings or statues, in accordance with the teachings of the Unified Church. These things were considered "primitive" and they were only seen in historic churches.

Since it was still early in the morning and none of the students had had breakfast yet, they were relatively quiet. Sister Elizondo led the prayers in a solemn, dignified way. Beto's mind drifted.

The previous night had gone well. He had walked alone on the beach under the stars with Adriana. They hadn't kissed or even held hands, but they had been alone and they talked for a long time.

Once morning prayers were over, Beto grabbed a

breakfast Nutribar and headed to his first period class. Beto knew Adriana wouldn't be in this Natural Science class, because she had taken it the year before with Gonzalo and Juan.

Mr. Stewart walked in the classroom and dropped a large canvas bag on his desk. Walking behind him with two big buckets was Marisa. The buckets looked heavy and Marisa looked tired. Her hair was messy. Her t-shirt had mud on it.

"Hey, new guy!" Marisa said, looking at Beto. "Stop staring and give me a hand here."

Beto jumped out of his desk and helped her lift the buckets onto a table in the front of the classroom. The buckets were filled with water and sea life.

"You won't be reading much from books in this class and your neuro chips will be next to useless, as they usually are," Mr. Stewart said. "I'll expect you to use your books as a reference in your projects, but this is going to be a hands-on experience."

He smiled at the class as he walked to one of the buckets, then reached in and pulled out a live fish.

"As long as you're near the ocean, you will always have a supply of good nutrition. Catching the fish, we'll do in another class. Today, we're going to learn how to get nutrition, tools, and other resources from a variety of ocean life."

"Miss Ramirez, please pick up that knife and clean this fish," he said as he slammed the fish down onto the table.

Marisa picked up the knife and stood looking at the

fish.

"I know it seems cruel, but believe me, the faster you kill it, the better it will be for this fish. Once it's been handled it has a very small chance of survival. And since it's going to die, it's our duty to make sure we use every bit of it."

Marisa stared at the fish. It was flopping around on the table, and looked like it might fall onto the floor at any moment. "I've seen diagrams of how to do this but I've never done it before," she said.

"Your life may depend on it someday," Mr. Stewart said. "You might as well learn to do it now."

Marisa still hesitated to touch the fish.

"May I?" Beto offered. "My brother lives in Louisiana and he taught me how to do just about anything having to do with seafood."

Mr. Stewart nodded. "Go for it, Louisiana,"

Marisa gladly handed the knife to Beto. He grabbed the fish with his left hand, thumped it hard on the table, then quickly cut its head off. He then delicately sliced open the belly and gently cut the guts out as the rest of the class winced. After a few more precision knife strokes, Beto laid the fish out on the table, well away from the guts and the head.

"We could grill it just as it is now," he said. "Or with a little more work I could debone it to make it easier to eat."

Mr. Stewart turned on a gas stove at his desk and pulled out a pan from the canvas bag.

"Do you have any oil for the pan?" Beto asked.

"You're not likely to have oil in the wild," Mr.

Stewart said.

"Well, the scales should keep the fish from sticking too much," Beto said.

"What about the head and guts?" Mr. Stewart asked. "What're you gonna do with them?"

"They're good fertilizer in the garden," Beto said. "They might work as bait."

Mr. Stewart was impressed.

"Well, Mr. Louisiana, I'm glad someone in this school has been taught a little bit of common sense. I don't see much of it in youngsters anymore."

Mr. Stewart reached into another bucket and pulled out what looked like a flat, gray rock.

"Can you shuck an oyster?" Mr. Stewart asked.

"With this knife? I don't know," Beto said.

"Give it a try while I put this fish on to cook," Mr. Stewart said.

The rest of the class period covered mussels, clams, crabs, shrimp, squid and crayfish. Everybody in the class got very dirty but they ended up enjoying most of the food. As they worked, they learned about the lifecycle of each creature, how to catch it, when to avoid catching it, and a million other details in Mr. Stewart's head.

By the end of the class, they were mentally overloaded and physically exhausted. They barely had time to wash their hands before the bell rang. Out in the hall, Marisa approached Beto.

"Thanks for saving me in there," she said.

"It was nothing," Beto said. "I've been doing that since I was a little kid."

"You really saved us all in there," Marisa said. "I've heard Mr. Stewart gets frustrated and angry with his classes because most kids know so little about what he's trying to teach. You actually had him in a good mood today."

"Thanks," Beto said, feeling very self-conscious.

"I guess Louisiana isn't your real name?" Marisa said.

"No. My name's Beto. Beto Gonzalez."

"Well, Beto Gonzalez, thank you for today," she said as she shook his hand. "Would you like to be my lab partner in Mr. Stewart's class?"

"Yes," Beto said.

"Great!" Marisa said. "We'll make a good team!"

Beto felt excited to be the lab partner for someone as charismatic as Marisa. And then he immediately felt guilty because he was kind of developing an interest in Adriana. But then he felt ridiculous because Adriana had done nothing but befriend him and his possibly romantic feelings seemed presumptuous.

The rest of Beto's morning went quickly. Sister Elizondo's religious history class was going to be the exact opposite of Mr. Stewart's class. "Lots and lots of reading," she had said. "We're covering one thousand years each semester." The list of books and articles that appeared on Beto's neuro chip was intimidating. But she sounded like an interesting teacher. Then it was back to Ms. Lin's class where Adriana and Gonzalo acted as friendly as ever, neither of them realizing how confused Beto was about their new friendships.

Then it was on to a half hour of student government

before lunch. Adriana stuck close to Beto as they found the rest of the sophomores on the bleachers in the gym. All of the classes had assembled, and Director Contreras was there as well.

The teacher giving the presentation was Ms. Yarlow. Beto had seen her working in the gardens with Mr. Stewart. He thought she was the English teacher for the junior class. She had fair skin and seemed to always look sunburned.

"I know it's the beginning of the year and you have a number of organizational details to attend to, but I wanted to bring you an issue that you may want to address, as the student government or as the entire student body."

The lights dimmed and the mini-jumbotron lit up. The oversized screen of the mini-jumbotron showed a beautiful sunset over the ocean.

"Perhaps some of you are aware that the south coast of Texas is home to a major sealife nursery known as the Laguna Madre. There are hundreds of miles of briny waters protected by our barrier island that are a perfect, safe habitat for young sea creatures.

"This area also sits over some significant uranium deposits. Several decades ago, some mining interests began extracting uranium, much to the displeasure of local inhabitants.

"The mining of uranium involves drilling wells to extract uranium-rich water, then removing the uranium, and replacing the water underground again. All this must be done without contaminating the Laguna Madre or the underground water sources that comprise our only water supply. And, even if it is done safely under regular conditions, you can imagine that everything gets more difficult when storms come through the region and flood the entire area."

Slides of geological formations went by quickly and Beto thought he was grasping a little of what was being said.

"We were fortunate that no major incidents occurred before the mining operations shut down more than two decades ago. There were some accusations of non-nuclear pollution in the drinking water, but nothing was ever proven.

"Now, however, the mining operations are planning to resume their activities. As coastal residents, I think we have reason to be concerned for our safety. But as a school, we have even more reason to be concerned. Our lease on this land can be revoked if the school were to lose something as critical as our water supply. The fact that we can access good drinking water from underground, even though we are surrounded by ocean, is an almost miraculous thing. However, if that water is tainted, the federal park service would love to close our school and take over this land."

"What can we do to stop them?" someone asked. It was a girl Beto had seen hanging around with Adriana named Gabriela.

"That is up to you," Ms. Yarlow said. "I will be writing and calling my congresspeople and senators. There will be local protests, I'm sure. I would like you to be knowledgeable about the situation and then take whatever responsible action you think is appropriate. The school will support you as much as we can."

"Uranium mining?" Adriana said. "That's crazy."

"We've got to stop it," Gabriela said.

Beto didn't know what to think. It certainly sounded scary. But what could go wrong?

Chapter 7 - Juan's Project

In which Juan proposes a project for the field lab and Beto gets off to a bad start with the lead teacher.

Adriana spent the rest of the student government time organizing her resistance to the uranium mine. Her arguments were reasonable, but also passionate. Her personal determination to take up this cause was inspiring, but she also began to lay out practical ways the student body could enact their opposition to the mining. By the time the thirty minutes was over, the sophomore class was convinced that Adriana should be their president for the coming school year. Then it was time for lunch, English, math, and finally class seminars.

In the seminar, Gonzalo and Juan grabbed Beto and claimed a table at the back of the room.

"Juan is ready to present his project," Gonzalo said. "We think it's good enough to earn us a place with the field laboratory this year."

"What is it?" Beto asked.

Juan was ready for this question.

"Remember the demonstration yesterday with the apples and the arrows?" Juan asked.

"Yeah, it was amazing!" Beto said.

"No, it was stupid," Juan said. "Bows and arrows and bow strings require years of training before someone can make them. And then years of practice before they can be used. And when you lose or break an arrow, you've lost hours of work. The bow and arrow is not the best hunting weapon to use for our purposes."

"What else is there?" Beto asked.

"The sling!" Juan said. "The same weapon the unarmored shepherd boy David used to defeat the heavily armed giant Goliath in the old Bible stories. All the sling requires is a simple leather or rope strap. The projectiles can be simple rocks."

"Can you hunt with a sling?" Beto asked.

"Better than with bows and arrows!" Juan said. "In 401 B.C. a Greek army of ten thousand, armed with bows and spears, was defeated by Persians with slings. The slings were deadly at ranges where bows could not even be used. In the Americas, the Spanish conquistadors reported that Incas could break a steel sword in half with a sling stone."

"But the Incas lost against the Spanish," Beto said.

"There were a lot of other factors involved in that war," Juan said, "but my point remains true. The sling has longer range and similar accuracy to the bow and arrow, and yet it is much easier to make."

"How do you know all this?" Beto asked

Juan tapped his finger against his neuro chip. "Books. Historical articles. I'll bet you could access some great videos with your NC3 chip. There is a lot of information about the sling."

"Do you know how to use it?" Beto asked.

"The idea is simple. Actually making it work will take some effort. But that's the project I'm proposing," Juan said. "The three of us will see how long it takes to become proficient in hunting with a sling."

"Are they going to let us starve to death if we don't catch anything with the slings?" Beto asked. "Because that sounds like something they'd do."

"Of course not," Juan said. "They'll feed us, right?"

Gonzalo looked worried. "I'll bet they will at first."

"That's all we need then," Juan said. "And then we'll know how to use the slings and we'll be fine."

"Have you ever gone hunting before?" Beto asked. "Because I have and even with a rifle it's hard to kill anything."

"The whole point of the field lab is to learn new things," Juan said. "No one is going to have it easy. This project is our ticket to get into the program."

"Where do we start?" Beto asked.

Juan pulled two long pieces of rope from his backpack. The boys spent the rest of the seminar class period on the beach slinging shells towards the ocean. The results were chaotic and not very promising. When the class period was over, Beto was ready to take a break. He had a lot of studying to do, but he had two hours until dinner. He could afford to take an hour off and let his brain rest.

But then his neuro chip told him to report to the first floor of the classroom building. He walked down the dark hallway past the faculty offices. One door at the end of the hallway was open. Gonzalo and Juan walked out of the door with mops in hand.

"What's going on?" Beto asked. "Why are you holding mops?"

An older man came out of the door after Gonzalo and Juan. He also had a mop in his hand.

"They're holding mops because they're going to mop every floor of this building," the man said. "And you're going to join them."

"Is this some kind of punishment?" Beto asked. "Did we do something wrong?"

"Is this some kind of punishment?" the man laughed. "No. Every student works. Every day. So get started!"

The man handed the mop to Beto and walked away. After a few steps he turned around. "Is this some kind of punishment? That's very funny. I'm going to keep my eye on you, Mr. Gonzalez. I think you might be a trouble-maker."

The man disappeared out the seaward exit. Gonzalo and Juan looked slightly shocked.

"You don't want to get Mr. Silva angry," Gonzalo said. "He owns us until dinner time. If he likes you, you might have some time off before dinner. If he doesn't like you, he'll work you hard until the minute dinner starts."

"I wasn't trying to cause trouble," Beto said. "I just didn't know we had to work."

"Everyone works. Every day," Juan mimicked the old man as he dipped his mop into the bucket.

Beto laughed. He didn't like the idea of doing

endless chores, but he was glad to have friends who were in it with him.

There were a lot of floors in the classroom building. The three boys started at the end of the first floor and gradually worked their way down the hall. The mop water filled up with dirty sand very quickly. The sea breeze blew the sand everywhere.

It was a hot day and Beto was sweating as he hauled the water bucket out the back door to dump the dirty water and get clean water every few minutes. Outside there were students mowing the grass and landscaping the grounds. Beto carried the bucket of clean water back up the steps and down the hall.

"What other jobs do students do?" Beto asked.

"Some work in the dining hall, serving meals," Gonzalo said. "That's a good job because you get plenty of food. The easiest job is being a teacher's aid. You get to sit around during one class period and do little things for a teacher."

"How did we get assigned to this?" Beto said.

"Juan and I did this last year and it wasn't too bad. At least we're indoors in the shade most of the time. We volunteered you for it so we could stick together."

"Thanks," Beto said as he pushed his mop methodically up and down a three-foot section of hallway.

The time went by very slowly. After half an hour they had worked their way halfway down the first floor, including the teachers' offices that were unlocked. The minutes dragged by.

After about an hour, Beto saw Adriana walking

down the hallway towards them. She had a slip of paper in her hand.

"Maestra Solis wants to talk to you three," Adriana said. "She was going to wait until you worked your way down to her office, but you're going too slow. She wants to see you now."

The boys propped their mops against the wall and obediently followed.

"What's your job?" Beto asked Adriana.

"I'm an aid for Maestra Solis after school. It's great 'cause I can get a lot of homework done."

Homework! Beto thought. *When am I going to have time to do all that reading for history and religion and English?*

The boys walked into Maestra Solis' office.

"It looks like you boys are working hard," she said.

"Yes, miss," Gonzalo answered.

"Are you enjoying the school, Beto?" she asked.

"Yes, ma'am. The students are friendly and the classes are very interesting."

Maestra Solis had a very calming personality. Beto instinctively trusted her. For some reason, she reminded him of home.

"I'm glad you're adjusting well," the maestra said. "Why don't you sit down? I'd like to talk to you for a few minutes."

The boys sat.

"Director Contreras has let me know that you three have submitted a proposal for the field laboratory. In fact, I have it right here. It looks very impressive. I have no doubt it will be accepted."

"Thank you, miss," Gonzalo said.

"But I'm worried about students going into the field lab too early," the maestra said. "Beto has only just arrived. He really needs to spend some serious academic time in classes to get the most out of the field lab."

"But, miss, he has the NC3 neuro chip. He is way ahead of us academically because of that. He has his class notes and his books right in his head all the time."

Maestra Solis smiled and nodded. "I know. I hear that from students all the time. But the neuro chip isn't magic. You still have to spend the time working with all that knowledge or you won't build on it."

"But, miss, we'll help him out there," Gonzalo said.

"I know you will, Gonzalo. But all three of you are so young. And Juan is so smart, he will do great things if he takes the time to do the academic work."

"So what are you saying, miss?" Gonzalo asked. "Are you not going to let us go?"

"I will let you go, but not this semester," the maestra said. "Prove to me you can excel at our academic requirements, and I will give you permission to go in the spring."

Gonzalo and Juan looked dejected.

"Okay, miss," Gonzalo said.

"And one more thing," Maestra Solis said, "I will agree to let you go in the spring semester, but in addition to this sling project, I'd like you to also do another project—one that takes a little more academic work."

"But you said you liked the sling project!" Juan said.

"I think it's a wonderful project. But I want you three to do more than spend a semester throwing rocks around the desert. You had a great project proposal last year that involved doing a plant survey, didn't you?"

Juan nodded.

"Do that as well, and get good grades, and do all your homework. Then I will give you permission to go out to the field lab."

"Okay, miss," Gonzalo said, looking much more cheerful. The three boys turned to leave the office and get back to work.

"Oh, Mr. Gonzalez, please stay here for just another minute," the maestra said.

Gonzalo and Juan disappeared.

"Have a seat," the maestra said.

Beto sat down.

"I'm a little surprised that after this school helped to get you out of trouble, that you are so eager to leave." Maestra Solis looked angry as she said this.

"I'm sorry, ma'am," Beto said. "I didn't even know about the field lab program until yesterday. And it wasn't my idea. Gonzalo just signed me up—"

The maestra held up a hand to stop Beto from speaking.

"Don't give me excuses. You've only known Gonzalo for two days. The decision you made was your decision and your responsibility. If you are going to continue at this school, I will expect you to take responsibility for your decisions."

"I understand," Beto said.

"And when you hear about something new and you have questions about it, come and ask me about it. As the lead teacher, I guarantee I know more about what goes on at this school than Gonzalo and Juan. They're good kids. You could have fallen in with a worse crowd. But you need to ask more questions before you start to dive into new things that you really don't understand."

"Then while I'm here, ma'am, I suppose I do have some questions about the field lab. Why does the school do it if you think it interferes with academic learning?"

Maestra Solis looked even angrier, although Beto was only trying to do what she had asked.

"Mr. Gonzalez, maybe in a day or two when I'm not so upset with you, I'll answer that question. Right now, please get back to work."

Beto truly didn't understand the level of emotion Maestra Solis was showing. He got up quickly and left the office. He wanted to stop and say he was sorry, but he couldn't think of how to do that in a way that wouldn't make things worse. Halfway down the hall, he heard Maestra Solis' door slam shut.

Gonzalo and Juan stared at Beto but said nothing. They worked in silence, finishing the rest of the first floor and moving up to the second floor. Mr. Silva walked by. "Don't forget to do the stairs," he growled. Beto picked up his bucket and walked to the bottom of the stairs.

The second hour of mopping was longer than the first. The smell of dinner was wafting down the halls. Beto was alone most of the time. How did he get in trouble so quickly at this new school? The lead teacher was already annoyed with him and he honestly couldn't figure out why. Finally, as the dinner hour approached, Mr. Silva came by and told them to put the mops away. He then disappeared down the hallway again.

When Gonzalo came down the stairs, Beto was staring at the wall.

"What are you doing?" Gonzalo asked.

"You know how there's a broom closet underneath those stairs at the end of the hall?" Beto said.

"Yeah," Gonzalo answered.

"And in the center stairway, there is open space under the stairs. But under this last stairway, the space has been closed in."

"So what?" Gonzalo said.

"It's strange. Why not use the storage space?"

Gonzalo shrugged. "I don't know, but I sure don't want to miss dinner. Let's worry about it later.

As they hurried to put the mops away, Beto nudged Juan. "Did you notice that?" Beto asked.

Juan nodded. "And I noticed even more. I'll show you later."

Chapter 8 - The Path in the Wilderness

In which a plan is revealed to sustain a small population in the desert for a long, long time.

The brown, dry desert seemed to stretch forever into the horizon. But down in the arroyo, there was shade and plants were green. Two women walked on the shady side of the gully until one of them, the older one, placed her hand on a boulder with crude marks scratched on it.

"This is it. The Mayan number for six—a solid line and one dot above it " she said, pointing to the scratches on the rock. "Smell the air. You can smell the moisture and the life all around us."

The younger woman smelled mud. And something grassy. Probably some plant she had stepped on.

The two women used two long, thin tree trunks to pry the large boulder away from the side of the arroyo. Once it rolled down and out of the way, the younger woman climbed into a crevice behind the place where the boulder had been. The other woman threw a number of large packages to the woman in the crevice. The younger woman stacked the packages neatly along a little ledge and then the women rolled the stone back.

"What do you think about this location?"

"It could flood. The water might make it as high as the boulder. A flood would definitely ruin the food. If animals don't eat it first."

"But the rock overhang gives us plenty of cover from the air. We could hide twenty or more people here. We just buried enough food to feed that many for a week or more. This high-tech packaging is designed to keep animals out. And there's a spring not far away."

"How far of a hike is it to location seven?"

"We can easily make it in one night."

"And then on through location twelve. Justo's goal was twelve waystations in order to survive for a year without outside support."

"That means they'll have to hunt for most of their food."

"That's the plan."

"And there's four of these trails? How many people is he planning to hide out here?"

"And for how long? He's been doing this for a long time."

The women sat in the shade and stared down the arroyo, to where the walls opened up to reveal the open desert.

"I don't think he's planning on going home."

Chapter 9 - Julia

In which Beto learns more about the Director's wife, Dr. Esquivel begins to explain her mission, and the campus is overtaken by refugees.

Beto did his homework until the lights went out. A little sign by his desk lamp said that the State Energy Board had mandated ten o'clock as the beginning of dark hours, except for emergency and public health purposes.

He found his way into bed by moonlight. He had already used his two minutes of water to shower earlier in the evening. He had hoped that since his roommate, Simon, was in the hospital with a snakebite that Simon's water allocation would still be available. A longer shower would have been nice considering how hot the weather had been. But the school had very efficiently taken Simon's water allocation away.

Nevertheless, the water had felt great on Beto's blistered hands. And it cooled down his hot, swollen leg that had been aggravated by his prosthesis. He wasn't used to all the standing and mopping. Beto was asleep within a minute of his head hitting his pillow.

The next day was much the same. Lots of new information. Lots of homework. Both Marisa and Adriana gave him lots of attention, which added to his confused feelings. And then the school day was over and time slowed down as Beto found himself mopping again. Mr. Silva had said mopping just one floor of the three-story building had not been enough the day before. The boys were told to work faster. Now they were on the second story, and it took longer to dump the dirty water outside. On the other hand, there was significantly less sand blown in by the sea wind. The second floor went quickly.

The three boys decided to see how quickly they could get the third floor done. Juan was assigned the stairwells. Gonzalo started at one end of the hall and Beto took the other end. Beto was making good progress and was looking forward to having a little time to relax before dinner, when he heard a voice coming from the director's office. It was Dr. Esquivel. She was talking to the director about the presentation she would be giving tonight to the entire student body.

And then Beto heard her say, "Tell me about Julia."

Beto froze.

"Why do you wish me to speak about that?" Director Contreras asked. "We're here to write the school's story, not mine."

"When the director of the school devotes an entire wall of his office to a photo of his beloved wife, who died in the nearby ocean... it's hard to believe the story behind all that doesn't affect the school."

"I see your point," the director said. "I have had

trouble leaving her memory in the past. But I don't see how psychoanalyzing me is going to help us."

"I'm not a psychologist. I'm a mythologist."

"What do you want to know?"

"Tell me about your marriage, your life together."

"We were very happy. We were going to travel the world together. But then her mother became ill. It was a very painful form of cancer. Julia devoted a year to caring for her, watching her as she changed from a healthy, happy woman into a scared, suffering wretch. It was difficult to watch. And then her mother died and we thought we would continue with our lives.

"Julia found an excellent teaching position. I was finishing my doctoral work. We were planning a hiking trip in Peru. And then she came home one day and said her doctor had diagnosed the same cancer in her that her mother had suffered from. Julia was paralyzed by fear. We thought perhaps the doctor could be wrong. But test after test showed the same results. Julia finished her first semester teaching and then she resigned from her job so that we could go on that trip to Peru.

"It would have been a wonderful trip except that we knew it would be our last. I have never felt so sad and so lonely as I was on that trip. Every moment I enjoyed with Julia only reminded me of how terrible it was to be losing her. She was brave, though. And cheerful.

"When we returned home, she said she would devote herself to fighting the cancer. She underwent aggressive measures. She ate all the right foods, exercised regularly, read all the right books, but the cancer continued to progress.

I could see in her eyes that she was remembering the pain her mother had suffered.

"One day I came home and found the note. She had bought a bottle of sleeping pills. She said she was planning to swim out to sea as far as she could go. We never found her body."

Gonzalo was waving at Beto, wondering why he wasn't working. Beto put one finger to his lips, signaling him to be quiet, and then pointed into the director's office.

"That is an amazingly sad story," Dr. Esquivel said. "And quite beautiful. And so you threw yourself into your work, eventually becoming the state teacher of the year. And now you have been awarded the headmaster position here."

"A few other things happened in between," the director said. "But that sounds about right."

"So, tell me, what does this school mean to you?" Dr. Esquivel asked.

Just then, Gonzalo lost his patience and yelled out, "Beto, what's going on here? Why am I doing all the work?"

The voices from the office fell silent, and Beto started mopping again. They managed to finish the third floor, but Beto had to run to get to dinner on time. There was a place next to Adriana, so Beto took it.

"Sorry I'm so sweaty," he said. "Work was tough again today."

"No problem," Adriana said. She was sitting with her friend Gabriela. Gabriela was a small, studious-looking girl—thick glasses, hair pulled back in a ponytail, and she was reading a real, physical book while she was eating.

"So, tonight, at the assembly, my goal is to draw Dr. Esquivel's attention to our environmental concerns," Gabriela said to Adriana. They were in the middle of this conversation when Beto sat down. *That is a good thing,* Beto thought, *I can focus on having enough time to eat before the assembly begins.*

"I think that will happen naturally, since the field lab program is so big at the school," Adriana said.

"But we have our three points that we have to make. The first is the opposition to the uranium mine. The state is already running out of water, we can't afford to contaminate what little we have."

Adriana was taking notes as Gabriela spoke.

"The second is habitat restoration for native animals. I think we should choose one animal to focus on. Ocelots are cute and they already have an organized group of concerned citizens working for them. It will be easy to tie into the efforts that are already being made."

"How do you spell ocelot?" Adriana asked.

Gabriela looked at Adriana's notes. "That looks close enough," she said.

"And the third point?" Adriana asked.

The bell rang. Beto was only halfway finished with his meal. He had to be in the auditorium in ten minutes. He took one last bite of his NutriVitaPro as Adriana grabbed his arm and dragged him out of the cafeteria. He dropped his tray in the recycling bin as they hurried to the assembly.

"I don't think you and Gabriela have officially met," Adriana said as they walked quickly. "Gabriela, you might be interested in the field lab project Beto is doing with his friends."

"The slings?" Beto asked.

"No, the plant survey."

"Oh, yeah. The boring one," Beto said. "We're supposed to be observing how the field lab project has impacted the native food plants we've been using."

"It's interesting because, on the one hand, you are digging up roots that take years to grow," Gabriela said, "but you're also clearing invasive plants so that the natives have more territory. I'm familiar with that project. I helped Juan Guzman write it up."

Beto nodded. "I think you and Juan may have a lot in common."

"He's a very focused student," Gabriela said. "I admire that."

They found seats near the front, which was important to Gabriela. It was only a moment before Director Contreras was on the stage. Students were still finding seats when he began to speak.

"Students, good evening. We have some important information for you. We don't want to interfere with your study time, but I want to explain a project I have in mind to strengthen our school. In order to do that, I've brought a celebrated scholar to our campus, Dr. Celeste Esquivel, to talk with you about who you think we are as a school and who we could be. Her scholarly work suggests that who you believe you are determines what possibilities you have in your future."

The auditorium remained silent.

"You look confused," the director said. "I will let

Dr. Esquivel explain."

Dr. Esquivel walked briskly up the steps onto the stage. The students applauded politely. Dr. Esquivel was relaxed, confident on the stage. It was clear that she was accustomed to speaking to large groups of people.

"Let me give you one example of how this works," she said. "More than seventy years ago, in the 1960s, the idea was placed before the American people that space travel to the moon was a possibility. At that time, we didn't have the technology to get into space. We didn't have the technology to leave the earth, much less get to the moon and land on it. We didn't know how humans could survive in the vacuum of space. But once people accepted the idea that their generation could be the 'Space Age,' that generation of Americans developed all the technology they needed for space travel in just about ten years. The idea, the mythos, came first. And then everything in the culture changed. The smartest people in the society were rocket scientists. The greatest heroes were astronauts."

The Voice began her commentary. "Okay, guys, she's *obviously* beautiful and that means you're probably going to believe *whatever* she says. But is she going to say anything more than 'If you can *believe* it, you can *be* it?'"

"But then things changed. A new national mythology began. Once we achieved the goal of space travel, people began asking what it was good for? Some people had the idea that the best way to explain to the American people the benefits of space technology was to show them how the new technology, developed for space, would also improve the lives of ordinary people back at home on planet Earth.

It wasn't long before that idea became the new national mythology. 'The wonders of science exist to make my life better.' And from that myth, a new age of personal fulfillment began. Americans became obsessed with health and wealth. The space program withered and died. The new race was for wealth. What followed was two generations of greed and self-service. Social injustice and environmental disasters were natural consequences."

"I'll give her points for social consciousness," the Voice said.

"Which brings us to *our* generation. Our new myth has become survival. With a damaged ecosystem and a world full of people who are angry that they have been exploited to produce wealth for a very small percentage of the world's population, how do *we* keep the natural world and the political landscape from ending billions of lives in our generation? The mythos of survival is why we have water rationing and electric-power limits everyday. It is why your parents cannot own private automobiles. It is why *every one of us* has a neuro chip directly connected into our brains so that we can most efficiently use our limited natural resources to fulfill the needs and desires of eight billion living people."

A hand shot up in the auditorium. It was Marisa, the Voice.

"What is the *next* mythos you see coming? You've mentioned 'the Space Age,' 'self-fulfillment,' and 'survival.' What's next?"

"Great question," Dr. Esquivel said. "That is what we are here to discover. What is likely to happen in your lifetimes? What do you hope to see?"

"Fewer people so we can all take longer showers," Marisa said. Laughter erupted in several sections of the auditorium.

"I agree. But I think that is still part of the 'survival' mythos. So what would come next once we have fewer people putting stress on our natural resources?"

Marisa was silent. She hadn't been ready for that question.

"The fact that you don't have a quick answer may mean that we aren't ready for the next mythos, the next step. But my work here will be to—"

Red lights began to flash in the auditorium. Director Contreras quickly excused himself and hurried to exit. Maestra Solis ran up onto the stage.

"We have an unusual emergency alert," the maestra said. "Director Contreras is going to check on it. For now, please stay in your seats."

Beto's neuro chip instructed him to "Please remain calm and await further instructions." Maestra Solis was concentrating hard on the information that was streaming into her neuro chip. "Oh, no!" she said aloud. She immediately began moving her hands and arms rapidly for no visible reason. This was a sign of an adult under a lot of stress trying to move lots of information around their neuro chip. Suddenly, students started moving. They were receiving the maestra's instructions. Adriana stood up.

"I have to report to the nurse's office," she said. "We are preparing for a medical emergency."

Beto's chip finally gave him more information.

"Report to the plaza immediately," it said.

Beto worked his way through the chaos and finally made it out to the plaza. Many students and teachers were already there. A man in a uniform was waiting for them.

"My name is Lt. Ivan Noriega of the U.S. Border Patrol," he said. "We have just intercepted a boat with quite a few people on it. They beached themselves trying to avoid capture. We have gathered them all up and they look pretty hungry and tired and scared. Your headmaster has agreed to let us use your school facilities until we can get enough vehicles here to transport them to our station. In the meantime, you can help by distributing a little food and water."

"Are these people dangerous?" a student called out.

"I think they're just tired and scared," Lt. Noriega said. "We're going to keep most of the students indoors out of the way and you guys are going to help me take care of these people. I have no reason to think any of them are dangerous. Most of them are women and children."

Beto saw dark forms walking across the grass from the beach. They walked slowly and seemed to have a defeated look about them. As they came closer he could see that they were all women and children. They wandered into the plaza and sat around the fountain.

"Do we have a student here fluent in Spanish?" Lt. Noriega asked. "My Spanish isn't great and none of these people have neuro chips."

Juan raised his hand, along with several other students.

"Okay then. You're going to help me explain to these

people that we're going to bring them food and water."

Juan translated this for the group of shivering people. "Vamos a dar a todos ustedes la comida y agua."

There were several sounds of relief and gratitude.

"Does anyone need medical care?" Lt. Esquivel said.

"¿Necesita alguien la asistencia médica?" Juan said.

Several people raised their hands.

"If you need medical care, please sit over here and the nurse will come to help you."

Beto helped two women and a large number of children move to the medical attention area. One child had a badly injured arm. Ms. Lin was helping Nurse Hannah, the school nurse, and she tried to keep the child comforted and calm while he waited for care.

More Border Patrol officers showed up and began asking questions of individuals. How long have you been in the boat? Where did the boat leave from? Do you know where the boat was going? Did anyone fall overboard?

At ten o'clock they were still trying to get everyone seen by the nurse. The plaza lights and all the lights in the building turned off.

"Does anyone have the authority to turn those lights back on?" an officer yelled out. Evidently no one did. They continued working by starlight.

Beto and Gonzalo took the children who were healthy to the soccer field and kept them busy kicking a ball around in the dark. A number of mothers who were also relatively healthy sat in the bleachers and watched. Many of them held babies in their arms.

"It's interesting how easy it is to see in the dark," Gonzalo said. "I've never been outside at midnight."

Beto looked around. It was true. The soccer ball and each person were easy to make out in the dim starlight. When people crowded together, the ball got lost in the shadows, but otherwise, it was easy to see what they were doing.

Adriana and Gabriela organized some students to bring water containers to the soccer field and they kept the children and mothers drinking.

"These people have been out in the ocean exposed to heat and sunlight for too long," Gabriela said. "The hallway around the nurse's office is filled with little kids suffering from dehydration."

Adriana and Beto kept encouraging the children to drink water. After a while, someone from the kitchen staff sent out snacks and the children eagerly accepted them.

Hours later Beto sat down next to Adriana and offered her half of a NutriVitaPro energy bar.

"Thanks," Adriana said. "Can you believe people have to live like this—risking their lives and the lives of their children to find a safe place to live?"

"It's terrible," Beto said. "What do you think will happen to them?

"I think they'll be deported. Most of them are from Guatemala."

"And they come here just to find work," Beto said. "It makes you realize how lucky we are."

Adriana nodded. "They are treated badly at home and then just as badly when they come here."

Eventually trucks arrived and all the visitors were driven away.

"It's time to go to bed," Maestra Solis said to the students on the courtyard. "You all were a great help tonight. Thank you."

The students began to leave for the dormitories.

"Beto, wait," Maestra Solis said.

Beto wondered if he was in trouble again.

"Beto, I was unfair to you the other day. I was in a bad mood and I took it out on you."

"Thanks," Beto said, not knowing what else to say.

"You are new here, and I shouldn't have assumed that you were trying to avoid academic work. We put such a high stress on the field lab, sometimes I feel like I'm fighting to keep students in class just to learn the basics before they leave and I lose them forever."

Beto nodded and stood in front of Maestra Solis looking uncomfortable.

"Can I ask a question?" Beto said, eventually.

"Of course," the maestra said. "I'm not going to snap at you like I did last time."

"How does this school work with college?" Beto said. "If so many students are doing field lab, what do colleges think?"

"Most of our students are smart enough to get good grades on the standardized tests. That assures colleges they know the basics. And colleges really love the field lab. They get really excited about it since it integrates so many different types of learning."

The maestra took a deep breath.

"I don't know, maybe I'm just too stuck in my ways. Maybe you guys do learn just as much outside the classroom as you do inside."

"Well, I've only been in class a few days, but I can honestly say the teachers here are amazing. I'm learning a lot."

Maestra Solis put her hand on Beto's shoulder.

"Thank you for saying that. Maybe I'm just having a mid-career crisis. You shouldn't have to worry about it, though. You just keep on learning in whatever way works best for you."

"Thank you, Maestra. Thank you for apologizing. I was really worried I had done something wrong, but I couldn't figure out what it was."

"I'll see you tomorrow. Get some sleep," the maestra said as she turned to go.

Beto headed for the boys' dorm. He was tired and ready for bed but as he walked through the shadows of the school buildings someone jumped out of the shadows in his way. It was Marisa!

Chapter 10 - Secret Passages

In which Beto and Marisa become convinced that there are secrets hidden on the school's campus.

"Just the person I wanted to see," Marisa said.

Beto was so surprised he could not say a word for a few seconds. Finally, he managed to get a sentence out.

"W-why were you looking for me?" Beto asked.

"As you might be able to tell by now, I'm a pretty intense person," Marisa said. "And I'm impressed by you. You did a good job out here tonight with the refugees."

"I was just trying to help," Beto said.

"And you didn't tell us that you had a criminal record," Marisa said. "What's that about?"

"How do you know about that?" Beto asked.

"Don't worry. No one is talking about you. I was able to figure it out from a couple of comments La Maestra made to El Director when she thought no one was listening. So, tell me about your criminal past."

"It's complicated," Beto said. "I broke the law, but then some cop beat me up. My family sued the city and we won the case, but it was really embarrassing for the police force and my parents thought it was best to get me out of there. For my safety."

"What'd you do?" Marisa said. "What'd you do that broke the law?"

"I hacked a personal vehicle and took it for a joy ride," Beto said.

"Cool," Marisa said. "Not the part about stealing a car, but being able to hack through the security system is impressive."

"That's what I was thinking," Beto said. "The cops focused on the theft."

"What was Maestra Solis talking to you about just now?" Marisa asked.

Beto had trouble shifting his mind to a new subject as fast as Marisa did. His mind was preoccupied with pondering why this smart, popular girl was talking to him alone in the dark. The fact that her mind moved so fast and she spoke so quickly did not help.

"Maestra Solis? What was she saying just now? Oh, nothing. We had a disagreement on my first day at school and she got mad at me. She was just apologizing."

"The *maestra* was apologizing to *you*?" Marisa said in wonderment. "The more I learn about you, the more impressed I am. Come with me!"

She took Beto by the arm and walked him towards the classroom building. Walking next to her, he could not help but notice that she smelled wonderful, like vanilla and lime.

"We're supposed to be going to our dorms," Beto

said. "They'll be taking roll and they'll miss us."

"I'm willing to bet they're too tired to worry about roll call tonight," Marisa said. "And there's something I want you to see."

She walked Beto towards the end of the classroom building closest to the girls' dorm. She stopped at the doors to the building.

"Juan said you noticed the enclosed stairwell," Marisa said.

"Yeah. So what?" Beto asked.

Marisa opened the door and walked to the stairs.

"If you look where the underparts of the stairway should be, they are closed in with brick. Well, the mortar around the brick looks different than the mortar of the rest of the building. You can't tell right now in the dark, but I think something is hidden in there."

Marisa's hands traced the mortar lines in the brick wall.

"What would someone hide in a school?" Beto asked.

"There are a lot of secret things going on," Marisa said. "They try to explain it away by saying they don't want resident students to be distracted by the weird things the field lab does, but I see a lot of people sneaking around."

"What do you think is going on?" Beto said.

"There are a lot of theories," Marisa said, as she tapped on the brick wall. "Getting in here could answer a lot of questions."

Beto felt the wall also. It felt like solid brick.

"Tell me one of the theories," he said.

"Well…" Marisa said. "Everyone agrees that Director Contreras is a little crazy. One theory says he's going to take all the students out into the wilderness and never bring us back. This school is his little nature cult and we're all being indoctrinated to turn our backs on society and to live in the wild."

"That actually sounds pretty good," Beto said.

"I know, I like it, too," Marisa said. "Sadly, I don't think the director is that crazy. Plus, how hard would it be to find us? The government has drones all over the place around here."

"And I think our parents would want to find us," Beto said.

"Maybe yours would," Marisa said. "Mine might be glad I was gone. But then again, they might come looking for me just to make sure I wasn't having too much fun."

Beto sat on the steps. He looked at the brick wall and couldn't think of how to find out what was hidden behind it.

"You and your parents don't get along?" he asked.

"They wanted a perfect daughter to match their perfect son. He's two years older than me. Instead they got a hyperactive, trouble-making kid who can never stop talking. I'm forever grateful to Director Contreras for saving me from them."

"Do you go home during the summer?" Beto asked.

"Unfortunately."

"You're from the U.S., right?" Beto said.

"Yep."

"Well, that's two of us."

Beto looked out the glass doors. The classroom

building joined at a right angle with the auditorium, so just to his left the outside wall of the auditorium extended out toward the sea.

"Just beyond this wall is the auditorium," Beto said. "Maybe there's a way in from the other side."

Marisa's eyes lit up with excitement.

"The entrance to the auditorium is on the second floor," Marisa said. "And the balcony area is entered from the third floor. So, whatever is through this wall is below the floor of the auditorium. We gotta go search."

"Good idea," Beto said, starting to stand up.

Marisa grabbed his hands and pulled him up. Beto felt an electric spark from touching Marisa's smooth hands. He wondered if this was a friendly touch, or something more. *Is she really curious about the building or is this like a date? And if it is like a date, at what point do I start worrying about how Adriana might feel about it?*

Marisa dragged him out to the plaza and they began to try all the doors to the auditorium. They found one that was unlocked down near the stage. They quietly walked into the dark auditorium. Marisa still had Beto by the hand and she pulled him up the side aisle. Halfway up the aisle, they heard a noise. Someone else was in the building.

"What do we do?" Beto whispered.

Marisa shrugged. Then she continued up the aisle, pulling Beto along. Beto tried to be as quiet as possible. They carefully opened the doors to the foyer. It was pitch black. Marisa stared into the darkness but could see nothing.

"Who's there?" a male voice said.

"Marisa," Marisa said.

"I should have figured," the voice said again. "Come on, Sara, it's getting crowded in here."

Antonio and a girl walked out of the foyer holding hands.

"We'll find some other place," Antonio said. He stopped in front of Beto. "The new guy? Is Marisa taking advantage of you?" he said, laughing.

"Ignore him," Marisa said, as she pulled Beto into the darkness.

"I feel bad about disturbing them," Beto said.

"Antonio and Sara can take care of themselves," Marisa said. "Besides, it's after curfew. They should be in their dorms."

"He's not going to turn us in, is he?" Beto asked. "Is he a student or a teacher here?"

"Good question," Marisa said. "He graduated last year and he's working in the field lab program. But he's obviously still dating his girlfriend, Sara, who is a student. That's totally illegal for a teacher."

"There are a lot of unusual things about the field lab," Beto said.

"Shut up and let's look for a way to get down below the floor," Marisa said.

They searched in the dark for anything obvious, but found nothing.

"We need light," Beto said.

"That would definitely get us in trouble."

"Where do you work after school?" Beto asked.

"In the field lab room," Marisa said.

"I clean the floors," Beto said. "Maybe I can come

in here tomorrow afternoon and look around while it's light. Can you meet me here?"

"Brilliant idea," Marisa said. "I'll be here."

They heard a sound outside the auditorium in the second floor great hall.

"Time to split up," Marisa said. She kissed Beto on the cheek and hurried down the auditorium aisle. *A kiss? First she held my hand and then a kiss?* Beto stood frozen with shock. But then he remembered Gonzalo's comment that a kiss on the cheek was just a friendly thing. And then he remembered that Gonzalo was from Mexico and Maria was from the U.S., so her kiss might mean something totally different. He shook his head to clear his thoughts. He was definitely dealing with stuff he didn't understand.

The door to the hallway shook as if someone was trying to open it. Beto heard Mr. Silva grumble to himself. Then he heard keys jingling together. It was time to go.

Chapter 11 - The Caretaker, Carlos Silva

In which Beto sees the "woman in white," the school population remains worried about the immigrant detainees, and the boys attempt to secretly enter the auditorium.

Beto made it back to his room, took his two-minute shower, and collapsed into bed. He was sound asleep when a noise from his open window awakened him. It was a noise he hadn't expected to hear—the sound of a young child laughing. He listened intently but he didn't hear it again. Had he been dreaming?

He got up and looked out the window, down into the courtyard. It was empty and quiet. In the darkness, he could just barely see the crests of the waves breaking on the shore. Then something caught his eye—a flash of white on the edge of the courtyard. There was a figure gazing out of the first floor of the classroom building. The reflections on the glass door made it hard to see, but he was sure someone was there.

Beto rubbed his eyes and took a second glance. If it was a person, it was someone in light-colored clothing. Suddenly, the figure turned and walked away from the door.

In that brief instant, Beto could tell it was a woman in a long, white dress, with straight black hair falling down the back of her dress.

Beto ran for his door. Barefoot, he moved quickly and as quietly as he could down the hall and one flight of stairs. His artificial foot clicked against the concrete. He ran to the closest door to the classroom building, but it was locked. He ran across the plaza to the next door, the door where the woman had been. It was also locked. These doors had been unlocked earlier when he and Marisa had examined the stairwell. He pressed his hands and face against the glass and looked down the hall in the direction the woman in white had been moving. The hallway was empty, as far as he could see. Whoever it was was gone.

Who would be in the classroom building in the middle of the night? Beto sat in the plaza, puzzling over this for a few minutes. Then he walked back to his room and fell asleep again.

When his neuro chip woke him up, he stumbled down to the dining hall. Everyone was still talking about the refugees from the night before. Beto wondered if the mystery woman could have been one of them? But no, he had seen them all driven away by the border patrol.

Earlier in the day, a student council member had posted a request on the neuro network for the students of the school to be kept informed of what was happening to the refugees. Maestra Solis posted that she would find out and share whatever information she gained with the students.

After breakfast, Beto stumbled into Mr. Stewart's class, tired from the night before. The natural science class was now starting to focus on native plants. Beto had a hard time staying interested. This made him worry that he had agreed to do a plant survey for the field lab. How was he going to be able to identify plants in the wild when he couldn't even do it in a class when they were clearly labeled?

Mr. Stewart held up two clumps of dried grass. They looked exactly the same to Beto. "Did you know there are more than five hundred species of native grass in Texas?" Mr. Stewart said.

Beto was terrified by this fact. This could end up being a long and tedious semester.

Sister Elizondo's class was taken over by another discussion of the refugees. Sister Elizondo herself was very eager to point out a number of biblical commandments to care for travelers, widows, and orphans. It was during this class period that Maestra Solis announced that the Border Patrol office had informed her that they could not discuss the status of the refugees, or detainees, as the Border Patrol called them. There would be no further information on where they were or what was being done to them. There was instantaneous outrage on the student channel of the neuro net. Maestra Solis promised to keep trying to find out something.

Ms. Lin was also preoccupied with the status of the refugees. She put a new saying of Master Kong on the board. "Look at the means a man employs, observe the path he takes, and examine where he feels at home. In what way is a man's true character hidden from view? In what way is a man's true character hidden from view? (Analects 2.10)"

"What is the true character of a nation that treats women and children like this?" Ms. Lin added. "These people came here seeking a better life and they were intercepted by armed officers and forced to make a dangerous nighttime landing on a deserted shore. And now they are being hidden by the government."

Juan raised his hand. Ms. Lin called on him.

"My father is an attorney," Juan said. "And legally the authorities cannot release personal information about detainees to the public. But the U.S. has the Freedom of Information Act, and we could probably get some information through that."

"Thank you, Juan. That is helpful," Ms. Lin said, and then she posted a notation on the neuro net to try the Freedom of Information approach.

"It is hard to know whom to blame for such suffering," she admitted. "But to witness such suffering and not respond would be inhuman."

The rest of the school day flew by for Beto. Soon, he was mopping the first floor again.

"Do we ever clean the floor in the auditorium?" Beto asked.

"Sometimes," Gonzalo said. "But it has carpet, so we have to use vacuum cleaners."

"Can we do that today?" Beto asked.

"Why do you want to clean the auditorium?" Gonzalo asked.

Beto gestured for Gonzalo and Juan to come closer. He then whispered what he and Marisa had discovered on the previous night.

"We've got to get in there," Juan said.

"Okay," Gonzalo agreed, "but Mr. Silva watches us pretty closely. We have to finish this floor fast and go to the second floor. Then, we'll go in the auditorium and say we thought it needed to be cleaned because of the assembly yesterday."

The boys mopped as fast as they could. It took just over an hour to complete the first floor. Mr. Silva came by as they were moving upstairs. He looked at their mopping job and couldn't find any obvious fault with it, so he said nothing. The boys watched him go outside towards the boys' dorm.

Beto quickly ran to the auditorium doors, only to find them locked.

"No luck," he said.

"They have to be able to push open from the inside, according to federal safety regulations. People have to be able to get out in case of fire," Juan said. "If we can find some way in, we could open these doors and claim they were unlocked when we found them."

"How do you know all this stuff about U.S. law?" Beto asked. "Your father is a lawyer in Mexico."

"He works on both sides," Juan said. "Many of his cases involve the U.S. in some way. People in Mexico with enough money to hire an attorney also have enough money to spend time in the U.S."

Gonzalo was already running upstairs to try the balcony doors. Not long after, he came down to report they were also locked.

"Let's try the outside exit doors," Beto said. "That's

how we got in last night."

But those doors were all locked as well. Then Gonzalo noticed a window that was slightly ajar high above them.

"What do you think?" he asked. "Could one of us make it through there?"

Beto looked at the old metal-framed windows. It would be a tight fit.

"Which one of us is the smallest?" he asked, knowing the answer was Juan.

Juan looked up. It was at least two meters up to the window. Getting up there and through the window was one problem, but he was more worried about what he would do on the other side.

"I think it's time for the human ladder," Gonzalo said. "Beto, you will be on the bottom. Brace your hands against the wall. I'll get on your shoulders."

The attempt to get inside might have worked except for the fact that the window to the auditorium was visible from the director's office. The boys were quickly detected and Mr. Silva brought the three boys up to talk to Director Contreras.

"Would you mind explaining what you were trying to do?" Director Contreras asked.

"We were trying to get into the auditorium, mister," Gonzalo said.

"I noticed that," the director said. "Why?"

"We clean the floors," Juan said. "I told Beto that the floor of the auditorium was larger than the floor of an entire story of the classroom building. He didn't believe me so we were trying to get in to measure."

"Why do you even care about that?" the director asked.

"We are given strict guidelines for how fast we ought to be cleaning," Juan said. "And since we used the auditorium last night we knew we would have to clean it soon. We wanted to be ready."

The director looked suspicious. Beto was impressed how quickly Juan was able to make up a somewhat plausible excuse.

"Next time, just ask Mr. Silva to open the door for you," he said.

Chapter 12 - The Night of Broken Glass

In which the students attend a county meeting to discuss the proposed uranium mine and violence brings the meeting to an early end.

As they left the director's office, Marisa was waiting for them. She punched Beto in the shoulder.

"I'm glad I wasn't five minutes earlier or I'd be in trouble, too," she said. "Or maybe if I had been there you guys wouldn't have tried such a dumb idea."

"Fortunately, the director was lenient on us," Beto said.

"What is your punishment going to be?" Marisa asked.

"He said he'd wait and let Antonio give us some extra work when we go out on the field weekend," Gonzalo said.

"That's not necessarily a lenient punishment," Marisa said. "Those weekends in the field can be tough."

Since it was now dinnertime, they walked towards the dining hall.

"And we still have no way to get into the auditorium

to search for a way into the underground," Beto said.

"And Mr. Silva's going to be watching us closely," Gonzalo said.

They arrived at dinner slightly late. Marisa was immediately pulled away into a group of other friends. The three boys got in line for their NutriVitaPro, in chicken form tonight. Adriana was waiting for them.

"Did you guys have a lot of work this afternoon?" she asked.

Beto wasn't sure if Adriana knew about the trouble they had gotten into, but he figured she was bound to find out one way or another.

"No," he said. "We got into trouble for trying to get into the auditorium."

"What were you doing that for?" Adriana asked.

The boys looked at each other, not sure of how much they wanted to reveal to Adriana.

"We were just curious," Beto said.

"Curious?" Adriana said. "About what?"

There was a guilty silence.

"Okay, don't tell me. It's not as important as talking about tonight's commissioners' court meeting."

Beto had no idea what Adriana was talking about. Adriana could tell by the lost look on his face that he was clueless.

"There is a county commissioners' court meeting tonight to hear public comment on uranium mining in the county. Students who are interested can go," she explained.

"Are we interested?" Beto asked.

"Yes, we are interested," Adriana said. "The

commissioners need to hear from the people who will be affected by polluted water if anything ever goes wrong with the mining operation. They need to see the faces of students like us who will suffer if this kind of industry is allowed to endanger our water supply."

"So this uranium mine could pollute our water?" Beto said.

Marisa nodded. "They say it's safe. But is it safe all the time? Is it safe if a major hurricane hits? Is it possible an employee can make a mistake?"

"I've been reading about it," Juan said. "It sounds pretty safe."

"Of course, that's what they are going to say," Adriana said. "But as Director Contreras says, one mistake and we could permanently lose our one and only water supply. Is it worth taking that chance?"

"Well, the county will make lots and lots of tax money from the industrial activity," Juan said, "and they don't make much from a not-for-profit school like ours."

Adriana glared at him.

"Anyway, while we still have a school, we are going to let our voices be heard," Adriana said. "Yes, they may make a lot of money going with industry, but they could be permanently sacrificing the educational and environmental uses of the land in the county."

They ate quickly, then Adriana herded them onto the school electrobus. Quite a few students were going. Dr. Esquivel was there, too. She was talking to Gabriela and some other students on the bus and taking notes. It was a long drive, just over an hour. The road along the island took them far north out of the county before there was a crossing onto the mainland where they could drive south again.

When they arrived, there were too many people to fit into the commissioner's court. People on both sides of the issue were crowded inside and overflowed down the courtyard steps into the street.

Beto was happy to be waiting outside. It was a warm night and the courtroom was hot and crowded. He and Adriana ended up sitting on the courthouse steps in the shadows where they could hear what was going on inside. From what they could hear, there were a lot of angry people on both sides of the issue. The mining proponents wanted the jobs and the income for the county. The opponents wanted to not have to worry about nuclear spills, contaminated drinking water, and ecological damage to the local fisheries.

Adriana was restless.

"What's wrong," Beto asked.

"I feel so useless out here," she said.

"Well, you got us all here," Beto said. "So people know we care about the issue."

"But we're not really *doing* anything," she said.

"At least Gabriela and Dr. Esquivel were able to get inside," Beto said.

"Yeah, and now that Gabriela has Dr. Esquivel's attention, she doesn't have time for me anymore."

She looked out at the courtroom grounds where some other locals were standing around holding protest signs. "We Want Clean Water!" "Don't Nuke Our Children!"

"Those guys out there have signs," Beto said. "With all the anger and yelling and stuff, they look a little crazy, but I can understand why they feel angry and scared."

"Maybe we should gather up all the students and go stand around with them," Adriana suggested.

"But then we couldn't hear what's going on inside," Beto said.

"Yeah."

The people speaking inside were saying the same things over and over, it seemed. And few of them were any good at public speaking. Then a rep from the mining company stepped up to the microphone. He sounded very reasonable and even a little friendly.

"Good evening, my name is Dr. Cruz. First, I want to say that I understand the concerns the local community has about our operations. And the community has every right to be concerned. In response, let me say that our company has a stellar record of compliance to local and federal regulations. We've been doing this kind of in situ recovery for decades with no dangerous accidents. It's a very safe process in which we pump carbonated water down to the uranium deposit. Then we pump the water back up and remove the uranium at very low levels. We reuse the same water over and over, and we take it all away when we're finished."

A long line of people began asking Dr. Cruz questions. He answered them all calmly and reasonably, Beto thought. It sounded like the uranium mine was winning the debate. And then Director Contreras came up to the microphone.

"Dr. Cruz gave us an excellent description of his company's operations. If you would like to read about those processes you will find very similar descriptions on your neuro chips, because that seems to be where Dr. Cruz's information came from. What he failed to tell you was the number of incidents on record in which local communities have complained about water supply contamination from this kind of in situ recovery.

"In fact, this happened the last time Mr. Cruz's company operated in this area. That matter is still in litigation. If the past can inform what we can expect for our own future, we may be facing suspicions of water supply contamination followed by years of very expensive litigation."

At this point, Mr. Cruz began yelling out responses to Director Contreras. This was followed by community members yelling responses to Dr. Cruz and the commissioners calling for order. The courtroom was eventually brought to order only to erupt again a few minutes later. Finally, the commissioners decided to clear the courtroom so they could discuss what they were going to do in response to this hearing. The county sheriff's department began escorting people out of the building.

Once outside, people began arguing again. The deputies were doing their best to keep the opposing sides away from each other. People were yelling back and forth and then there was a loud crash—the windshield of one of Dr. Cruz's trucks shattered.

A woman screamed and the crowd began to scatter. The deputies immediately began clearing people off the courthouse property. More sheriffs' vehicles began to arrive. Maestra Solis began grabbing students and putting them back on the bus.

"Was that a gunshot?" Marisa asked, as she was pushed onto the bus.

"Just get in your seats and keep your heads down," Maestra Solis said.

Adriana and Beto climbed into the bus and were pushed to the back as more students piled in. They claimed the very back bench and sat, heads down, waiting for the next thing to happen. The bus was full of chatter.

"I don't think the bus will stop bullets," the Voice said. "But just keep calm and do what the maestra says."

"Keep your heads down in case the glass breaks!" the maestra yelled.

The bus driver had the electric engine on and was ready to go. The adults counted the students. Two were missing. Beto looked around.

"Where are Gonzalo and Juan?" he said. "Has anybody seen them?"

Moments later, the director appeared with the two missing boys.

"We're all here, now," he said. "Let's go. Everyone keep down and keep quiet"

The bus drive back to the school was silent. After they had left the town and were on the highway, Maestra Solis stood up.

"You've just seen an interesting example of the political process. Our elected officials had an open meeting to hear the concerns of the community about an important issue. People were allowed to speak freely. Unfortunately, the argument got heated and the public meeting was cut short. And then, there was the broken windshield. The deputies said it was not a gunshot as was rumored, but a rock someone had thrown."

The maestra paused, at a loss for words.

Director Contreras continued. "Tonight, we saw both the good and the bad of local politics in this country. In my experience, it usually isn't this exciting. But it looks like no one got hurt and no one has ended up in jail."

"What happens now?" Marisa asked.

"Now, the county commissioners will decide whether to grant the permits for the mining operation," Maestra Solis continued.

"And that's it?" Marisa said. "They get to decide?"

"As long as the mining company complies with all the laws and regulations, they will be allowed to operate like any other business, if that is what the commissioners' court decides," she said.

"Even if it's dangerous to the people who live around the mine?" Marisa said, frustrated.

"If people think the decision of the county is inappropriate, they can bring the matter to court. But they have to be able to show that some regulation or some law is being violated."

"And if our water is ruined?" Marisa said.

"We have to hope that doesn't happen," the maestra said. "But we'll come up with a plan just in case that happens."

The maestra sat down. Most of the students began to relax. Beto could tell that Adriana was still frustrated. Dr. Esquivel began talking to the students around her again. Director Contreras sat in the very front of the bus, scowling.

When they arrived at the school, the students were sent to their dorms. Adriana took Beto's hand.

"Thanks for coming," she said. She squeezed his hand and let go.

"It was interesting," Beto said. "Thanks for inviting me."

As he walked towards his dorm he noticed that the director was standing by the bus talking to Gonzalo and Juan.

In his room, Beto lay in his bed quietly listening for the sound of Gonzalo and Juan coming back to their room. He was almost asleep when he finally heard their door open. Beto got up and ran into the hall.

"Hey! What took y'all so long?" he asked.

His two friends were silent for a long moment.

"You better come inside," Gonzalo said.

Beto followed them into their room and Gonzalo closed the door. Beto looked from one to the other waiting for an explanation.

"I broke the windshield," Juan said.

"What?" Beto said. "Why?"

"It's hard to explain," Juan said. "I had been practicing with the sling for a few weeks, and I've never hit what I was aiming at before. And then I thought I'd throw a rock at the truck. Not to break anything, just to show a little anger towards the mining company. And no one was near the truck. It was by itself on one side of the parking lot. And then the sling actually worked, unexpectedly. I swung it around and the rock shot out like a bullet. It went straight through the glass."

"And what did the director say?" Beto asked.

"He was mad, of course," Juan said.

"Really mad," Gonzalo added.

"He's deciding what to do," Juan said. "I might get kicked out of school."

Chapter 13 - The Questions

In which Beto and Adriana face the questions of Dr. Esquivel.

It was a long night for Beto. He couldn't believe Juan had done such a stupid thing. And he couldn't believe Juan might be sent home.

By the time breakfast started, all three boys were miserable with worry and lack of sleep. When the bell for first period rang, Juan was called to the director's office.

"What's going on with him?" Adriana asked.

"I can't say. But I think we'll know soon," Beto said.

They split up and went to their classes. Dr. Stewart's Natural Science class had finally gotten beyond grasses and other boring plants. They were now working with edible plants. Beto and Marisa watched a yucca root roasting in a toaster oven. Watching the root cook was not very interesting, but Beto was enjoying standing close to Marisa. Gonzalo was trying to make thread from the yucca leaves.

"That was quite a night last night," Marisa said. Her hair was so close to Beto's nose that he had no choice but to take in her familiar scent. It was intoxicating.

"It was definitely more exciting than I was expecting," Beto said.

"Do you really think that was a rock that somebody threw? It sounded like a gun to me," Marisa said.

"I'm pretty sure it wasn't a gun," Beto said.

"But that windshield just exploded," Marisa said. "That was some throw!"

"Big crowds like that make me nervous," Beto said. "And everyone was so angry. I was glad to get away."

"I kind of liked it, in a strange way," Marisa said. "Here in the U.S., we're always being told how the rest of the world is out of control. It seemed like a little bit of poetic justice to see people here lose control so quickly."

"It's definitely not perfect here," Beto said. "And I think all the water and fuel rationing has made people more angry, in general."

Beto's neuro chip alerted him to a message from the director: report to the the office immediately.

"What's wrong?" Marisa asked.

"It's the director. I've got to go," Beto said. He wondered if Juan's troubles had somehow involved him again. He hurried to the third floor, where Juan was sitting on a bench outside the office. Oddly, Juan was smiling, but he said nothing. He just pointed to the director's door. Beto knocked on the frame of the open door. The director signaled him to come in.

"Yes, sir," Beto said.

"Mr. Gonzalez. You have teamed with Mr. Huerta and Mr. Guzman to do a sophomore field lab project."

"Yes, sir." Beto said. "We submitted two projects, actually."

"Right. Well, I have good news for you. The projects have been approved."

Beto was surprised. One minute Juan was in trouble and now his project was approved.

"We have made some modifications on the schedule, however," the director continued. "Maestra Solis would like for you to spend more time in the classroom, so we are approving your projects for the spring semester. However, you will be required to attend the field lab orientation for three days starting this weekend. Will you be able to do that and keep up with your classes?"

"Yes, sir," Beto said.

"Do you have any questions?" the director asked.

"I don't think so, sir."

"No questions at all?"

Beto paused. "No, sir."

"Do you wonder why Juan is being allowed to go out with the field lab in spite of his trouble last night?"

"Actually, sir, I was wondering that."

"Did you have anything at all to do with this incident?"

"No, sir. It surprised me. I'm pretty sure Juan was even surprised by it. He said he had never hit what he had been aiming at before."

"Juan assured me that you had nothing to do with it," the director said. "I just wanted to hear that from you. I am inclined to think the incident arose from a young man being a little too enthusiastic practicing for his project, coupled with making a very bad decision at a very bad time. If anyone had connected Juan to that event, it could have been very embarrassing for this school."

"I understand, sir." Beto said. "Are you going to tell anyone what happened? Like the police?"

"Maestra Soils and I are discussing the best way to let the authorities know what happened. You don't have to worry about that. But please help to make sure nothing like this ever happens again. The field lab has many opportunities to interact with people in the outside world and it is imperative that all of your interactions be positive. It is not just your reputation on the line. It is also the school's."

"I certainly understand that, sir."

Beto was feeling very pleased that Juan was not in serious trouble and they would all be able to go into the field. And Maestra Solis had satisfied some of her demands as well. Somehow, making Maestra Solis happy was important to Beto. Maybe being so far away from home, he needed a mother figure in his life. He promised himself he would do well in his academic studies. This was turning out to be a good day.

"There is one more thing," the director said.

Beto smiled and listened.

"Juan will face some punishment, to make sure he fully understands how close he came to disaster, for himself and the school."

Beto nodded.

"As his partners, you and Mr. Huerta will take part in Juan's punishment. I expect you to act and take responsibility as a team from now on."

"Yes, sir." This was not sounding as good as Beto had hoped.

"Your punishment will be assigned to you by Antonio Reyes this weekend. I assure you it will teach you a lesson that you won't soon forget. Are you willing to fully accept this responsibility as part of Mr. Guzman's team?"

Beto paused, trying to imagine what the punishment might be. "I will, sir," he finally said.

"Excellent," the director said. "And now, I'd like you to take a few minutes to meet with Dr. Esquivel, so that she may interview you before you leave. Please report to her in the first floor reception area."

"Yes, sir," Beto said. "I promise I'll do what I can to keep our team out of trouble."

The director looked and him, and almost laughed. "I have had to speak to you twice about your behavior in the brief time you've been here, Mr. Gonzalez. You have a degree of enthusiasm that could make you a very good student. Or it could get you into trouble. I am giving you this chance to prove to me that you can make the decisions necessary to channel your enthusiasm in a positive direction."

"I understand, sir."

The director went back to his work and Beto hurried out of the office where Juan was waiting for him.

"What do you think?" Juan said.

"It sounds like we're going to be watched very closely," Beto said. "But it sounds great!"

They went their separate ways. Beto hurried down to the first floor, where he saw Adriana waiting in the reception area.

"What are you doing here?" Beto asked.

"I'm here for an interview with Dr. Esquivel," Adriana said.

"Me, too," Beto said.

"I know. She interviews students in pairs. I scheduled us together."

"Cool. Thanks," Beto said.

"Gabriela couldn't get out of class today," Adriana said, smiling. "You were my second choice."

"Well, that's still pretty good," Beto said, smiling back. "Second choice isn't too bad."

He sat down on a wooden chair facing the big, cushy chair Adriana was in. It wasn't long before Mrs. Mendoza told them Dr. Esquivel was ready for them.

They walked into a small office where Dr. Esquivel was sitting at an old wooden desk. A window looked out onto the plaza. Dr. Esquivel was wearing glasses and her hair was pulled back into a ponytail. The desk was covered with papers. A camera sat on the desk facing the students.

"You are Adriana Cavazos Aguilar and Roberto Gonzalez?" she asked.

The students nodded.

"I'm Celeste Esquivel. Please have a seat," she said. "I apologize for this ugly little office," she said, "but it's the quietest place I could find."

Adriana and Beto sat in the two wooden chairs.

"I'm going to ask you three questions. From these questions, I hope to discover the underlying mythology of this school. These questions aren't a big secret, but I will ask you to not share them with anyone until after I'm finished interviewing. I think the process works best when people haven't had a whole lot of time to think about the questions."

Adriana and Beto nodded and sat quietly. Dr. Esquivel smiled. She had a warm smile, Beto thought.

"Okay. First question. What do you want to do with your life and what does being at this school have to do with that?"

Beto looked at Adriana and it looked like she was ready for this question.

"I'd like to study medicine," she said. "I'm here to learn English and because there are better educational resources in this country to get me established in my career. However, eventually I want to live and work closer to my family."

"And where is your family?" Dr. Esquivel asked.

"Veracruz."

"Interesting," Dr. Esquivel said. "So you want the best education you can get but you don't want to lose your connection to home and family?"

"Of course," Adriana said, as if anything less would defy logic.

Dr. Esquivel looked at Beto. "How about you?"

Beto shrugged. "I'm just a sophomore. I'm thinking about engineering."

"And why did you come here?"

Beto looked even more uncomfortable. "I got in trouble back home, so I had to go somewhere else. This school looked like a good school, plus it was in an isolated area where I might be able to stay out of trouble."

Dr. Esquivel smiled. "That sounds like an honest answer, but it also sounds more like it might be your parents' perspective. Why did you agree to come here? Is there anything that appealed to you?"

Beto thought for a moment.

"The international student body," Beto said. "To live with people from other cultures seemed very interesting. And the natural setting. I like being surrounded by nature instead of a big, ugly city."

"Wow. Those are good reasons," Dr. Esquivel said. "The international community matches a little with Adriana's desire to have bigger opportunities than those that were available back home."

She looked at Adriana to see if she agreed. Adriana nodded.

"Although Veracruz is a major city," Dr. Esquivel said. "And the natural setting. You didn't mention that, Adriana."

"It is pretty here, but Veracruz is prettier," Adriana said. "We have much better beaches. And I miss the city. It's too wild out here. There are so few people."

"You feel a little isolated?" Dr. Esquivel asked.

Adriana nodded.

"But the isolation sounded like a good thing from your perspective, Beto. True?"

"Mostly. I'm okay with being away from the city."

Dr. Esquivel wrote some notes. Beto was surprised that the older generation still used paper. It seemed like such a cumbersome way to organize thoughts.

Dr. Esquivel brushed a loose lock of hair behind her ear, and Beto noticed that he was watching her closely. It was easy to be enchanted by her intense passion for her work. Discomforted by this thought, Beto looked out the window.

"And now for the second question," Dr. Esquivel said.

Even her voice was captivating to Beto. Her slight accent made every word seem interesting.

"If you could take a class on anything, any topic you could imagine, what would it be?" Dr. Esquivel asked.

"Piano," Beto said, instantly. This answer surprised even himself. "I haven't studied music. But I'd love to be able to make music."

"I didn't know that about you," Adriana said.

"How is the music program here?" Dr. Esquivel asked.

Adriana shook her head. "There is none. The old school has a choir, but here, I guess we're just starting. So, we have no music. We have just the basic academic courses. And the field lab, of course."

"How do you feel about the lack of a music program, Beto?" Dr. Esquivel asked.

"I hadn't really thought about it. I think of music as something fun I'd like to do someday. School is for the boring, day-to-day things you have to do so you can get a job."

Dr. Esquivel started writing really quickly, and smiled. "That's a very interesting perspective, Beto," she said. "You don't think that work and enjoyment of life go together?"

Beto thought about this for a moment, then shook his head. "Nope. Work is what you have to do to survive. It's what society demands from you. Enjoyment is what you do for yourself."

Dr. Esquivel wrote some more. "You and I need to talk again after you've been at this school a little longer," she said. She then shifted her gaze to Adriana. "And you, Adriana? What would you like to take a course in, if anything was available?"

"I don't know," Adriana said. "If I could do anything at all, maybe learn to fly."

"Fly? As in airplanes?" Dr. Esquivel asked.

"Yes. I had an uncle who was a pilot in the Air Force," Adriana said. "Flying sounded wonderful. Back when people did it often."

"There is still a need for some pilots," Dr. Esquivel said. "The commercial airlines are gone, but being a pilot is still an option."

"It's just a dream, not a practical thing," Adriana said.

Dr. Esquivel nodded. "I actually remember flying a lot when I was young, before the fuel conservation efforts. The big airplanes were actually pretty uncomfortable. People were packed together like animals. Actually, probably worse than animals. I don't think animals would tolerate that kind of treatment. Traveling by ship is much more civilized."

She wrote a few notes.

"Music and flying," she said, smiling. "Those are

both beautiful aspirations. You two are very good with these questions."

Beto noticed how that little bit of praise allowed Adriana to relax a little. She had been sitting very stiff and formal. Now she was smiling and more animated.

"And now for the last question. What is the absolutely best thing that has happened to you at this school?"

Adriana's eyes shifted to the ceiling, evidently thinking hard.

"I think it has been the opportunity to study very hard and very seriously," Adriana said. "I feel like I'm learning a lot here. We read a lot and research a lot. I'm being pushed harder to learn than I would have been if I had stayed home."

"Wow, that's interesting," Dr. Esquivel said. "A student who appreciates being pushed hard to learn. That's very exciting to hear. I'll have to tell my own students how lucky they are when I push them hard."

Adriana laughed. Dr. Esquivel turned to Beto.

"For me, the best thing has been making friends," he said. "Adriana and Gonzalo and Juan—they are the friendliest people I've ever known. I've only been here a short time, but they have really made me feel like I belong here."

"That's wonderful," Dr. Esquivel said. "Schools like this can be very lonely or threatening for some students. I'm very glad to hear you feel welcome here."

Beto and Adriana left the meeting with Dr. Esquivel feeling great about themselves and the school. However, as soon as Adriana left to go to her next class, Beto saw

Antonio Reyes standing in the hall waiting for him.

"Beto Gonzalez," Antonio said. "You have not even started with my field lab and you are already in trouble. I promise you that you are going to suffer this weekend. You are going to suffer because, in my field lab, I cannot afford to have troublemakers. I will either make you suffer so much you will never again come to the field lab or you will come and never dare to get into trouble again. Do you understand what I'm saying?"

"Yes, sir," Beto said.

Chapter 14 - The Field Lab

In which Beto is introduced to life in the field lab.

For the next two days, there was nothing that could make Beto happy. Marisa was excited he was coming to the field lab with her. Adriana congratulated him for being accepted into the program. Mr. Stewart gave him field guides of plants to look for that would impress his teachers. But all Beto could think of was Antonio's promise—that he would suffer this weekend. It was obvious that Antonio had had a similar conversation with Gonzalo and Juan, because they were also walking around with looks of terror in their eyes.

The three boys packed exactly what they were instructed to pack, which was almost nothing. Then, at the appointed time, they waited at the large flagpole on the western side of the island. All the field lab students were gathering there. Along the sandy beach were dozens of two-person kayaks.

It was a few hours before sunset when they saw a kayak approach the coast from the west. As the kayak came closer, they saw Antonio and another person paddling through the waves coming toward shore.

A tall, muscular woman separated herself from the group of students.

"That's Rosario Gomez," Marisa whispered to Beto. "She's Antonio's second-in-command."

"Listen up, people!" Rosario said. "We are now beginning your introduction to the field lab. The first thing you will do is turn off your neuro chips. We want you to get used to thinking and acting based on your own judgement, without outside aid. Later on, if your project requires that you have access to the neuro net, we may approve that on an individual basis. But for all of you this weekend, turn your neuro chips off!"

The students all complied. Beto's neuro chip gave him one final warning before powering down. *Are you sure you want to power down? All safety functions, even in case of emergency, will be unavailable.* Beto gave the mental command, "Yes." He felt an emptiness in one part of his brain as the neuro signal stopped. He felt isolated and began to wonder how he would know if something went wrong somewhere in the world.

Rosario continued her instructions, pointing out to the kayak that was still approaching.

"Watch closely how that kayak is being paddled. The two people paddle on opposite sides of the kayak. They dig deeply into the water with each stroke. They keep a steady pace."

Beto noticed how strong Antonio's arms were as he paddled closer and closer to shore.

"The person in back is in charge of steering the kayak. He or she will keep the kayak aimed exactly perpendicular to the waves, so that your kayak cuts through each wave. If you turn parallel to the waves, they will throw you around and turn you upside down. It is imperative that the person in back maintains the correct direction in reference to the waves."

Antonio's kayak was doing exactly what Rosario described—it cut through each wave it encountered.

"Antonio and Luis will hit this beach in just a few minutes. From the time they land, you will have less than five minutes to get into your kayak and be ready to begin paddling to the mainland. You will not enter your kayak until it is floating in the water. However, right now, you will stand by your kayak. You will clip your baggage securely onto your kayak. You will have two liters of water, also clipped securely to the kayak. Do it now!"

People began pairing up and hurrying towards the kayaks. Gonzalo, Juan, and Beto did not know how to divide up until Marisa grabbed Beto and ran with him to the nearest available kayak. They clipped their gear to the little boat.

"It is two miles to the mainland. We should all make it there in less than an hour. You will stay with the group, and you will paddle at the pace Antonio and Luis set for you. Remember, they have already paddled two miles, so you have no excuse for not keeping up with them.

"I suggest you put the heaviest and strongest person in the rear of the kayak. I do not want to see any tiny people in the back. You will not make it to the other side if you are bow-heavy."

Antonio's kayak was coming in very close to shore.

"At this time, each person will put on their life jackets or, as we call them, your portable flotation devices— your PFDs. You will wear a PFD any time you are in your kayak."

Beto put on his PFD and he felt like a giant marshmallow with pale, skinny arms sticking out the sides. Antonio and Luis were also wearing PFDs, but the two men were so muscular, he hadn't noticed the life jackets on them from a distance.

"If you stray from the group, or if you cannot keep up with the group, I will come and paddle alongside you until you make it to the mainland. However, you do not want to become known for laziness or weakness during your time with the field lab, so I suggest you do all you can to stay with the group."

Antonio's kayak slid onto the sand.

"Listen up! Do not mount your kayaks yet!" Rosario yelled, as some students started to move into the water. "Your safety briefing is not over!"

The students sheepishly exited the water.

"One and a half miles across this stretch of water you will notice a string of sand bars to your left and right. When you cross those sand bars, you will be entering the inter-coastal waterway. This is where boats and ships go up and down the coast. These ships are big enough to crush you without even noticing you are there. We will all gather together at the sand bars. And then Antonio will lead us across the last half mile in a very tight group. This will be the most dangerous part of our trip. You will stay close together. We will have staff members on our right and left with very bright lights. At no time will you ever let your kayak leave the group. You will never go beyond the kayaks with the bright lights. Is that understood?"

"Yes, ma'am!" everyone yelled.

"Then grab your paddles, launch your kayaks into the water, and mount up!"

Chaos ensued. Students splashed and kayaks ran into each other. A few students fell into the water as they tried to mount their kayaks. Marisa told Beto that he would be taking the rear position. They mounted with relative ease, except that they ended up parallel to shore and the waves began to rock them immediately. They took a few seconds to figure out how to get the kayak turned the right way, and they were off.

Steering was a challenge at first. Kayaks were weaving all over the place, but it wasn't long before everyone got the hang of it. And then the challenge was to keep paddling at Antonio's pace. It was easy to do for a little while, but Beto quickly realized this quick pace was going to have to be maintained non-stop for the next hour. His arms immediately began to feel weak and his muscles began to burn with the effort. But Antonio did not reduce his pace. Beto dug his paddle in the water over and over. He did not want to be the first person to fail.

After about ten minutes, one kayak began to lag behind. Rosario immediately moved next to it and began yelling at the paddlers.

"How are you doing?" Beto yelled to Marisa.

"My arms are hurting!" she yelled back over the splash of the waves hitting the bow. However, she did not let up her pace.

"Mine, too!" Beto said.

They continued to paddle as the coastline receded farther and farther from them. The far coastline did not seem any closer. Then Beto's paddle hit sand. The water was only inches deep.

"This is a sandbar," Rosario yelled. "Keep paddling until we get beyond it. Do not get out of your kayaks. There are stingrays in the water and you do not want to step on one of them."

Beto kept paddling. At one point, the kayak was actually scraping across sand, but they managed to push beyond that section with their paddles. Soon, they were afloat again and they could no longer see the sand through the murky gulf water.

The paddling seemed to go on forever. Beto watched a barge pass in front of them as it traveled south on the inter-coastal waterway. Not long after that he saw fins to his right.

"Dolphins!" Marisa shouted.

Beto was relieved they weren't sharks. He steered slightly towards the dolphins, but they quickly disappeared.

And then it was more paddling. Beto was soaked with sweat and his back was aching when he finally caught sight of the line of sandbars that marked the edge of the waterway. But they did not seem to be coming any closer as he paddled. Over and over, he dug his paddle into the water and yet the distant shore seemed to draw no closer. Marisa began to moan with fatigue.

"I'm so tired!" she complained. She kept paddling, but her strokes were less smooth and less strong. It took more effort for Beto to steer.

Finally, far ahead, Antonio's kayak reached the sandbar. Antonio jumped off his kayak and stood up. All the kayaks began to turn towards him. Beto looked back and could see a few stragglers far behind him, being shepherded by the angry Rosario. He was glad he wasn't back with them.

He paddled and paddled and paddled and finally Antonio seemed to be getting closer. Eventually his kayak hit sand and most of the kayaks were together in a tight group.

"Stay in your boats and rest a little," Antonio instructed.

The remaining kayaks caught up a few minutes later.

"I'll give you all a minute or two to catch your breath, and then we will all cross together," Antonio yelled.

Beto looked up and down the channel. There were no ships in sight. The sun was getting lower over the far shore. Marisa drank some water. Beto did the same.

"Are you okay?" Marisa asked.

"I'm tired, but I'm okay," Beto said.

"Me, too."

Beto was impressed by Marisa's strength. Her arm muscles were pretty well-toned. He hoped he could keep up with her.

Before he really felt rested, Antonio was back in his kayak and the group headed into the inter-coastal waterway.

Antonio paddled a little less aggressively. He obviously wanted the group to stay together. The water was a different color here. It was much deeper and the depth gave the water a darker, bluer hue.

It wasn't long before Beto could see the far shoreline coming closer. And then he saw a flagpole that seemed to be the point to which Antonio was aiming. Before long, they landed on the mainland. Rosario was already there, yelling out instructions.

"Pull your kayaks ashore. Unclip all your personal gear. Fasten your paddles and PFDs to the kayak. Then drag your kayak across the sand and set it down in the grass. Why do I want the kayaks in the grass?"

Rosario looked around, waiting for an answer.

"Because you don't want them to float away at high tide," Juan answered.

"That's right," Rosario said. "But be careful in the grass. You do not want to surprise any snakes. Make sure they hear you coming and they have time to get out of your way. I promise you, they will get out of your way if they can."

Beto and Marisa carefully pushed their kayak into the grass.

"Watch out, snakes!" Marisa yelled, playfully.

Once all the kayaks were positioned, Antonio led the group inland along a well-worn path. The path wandered through the grass until a large sandy opening appeared.

"This will be home for the next three days," Antonio said. "You will have no tents and no sleeping bags. You will sleep on the sand. You will be stung by mosquitoes. The burning hot sun will fry your skin if you are stupid enough to expose yourself. Once the sun rises in the morning, you will all be wearing a long sleeve shirt, long pants and a wide-brimmed hat. In addition, you will wear a handkerchief over the back of your neck and closed-toe shoes. Does anyone not have the clothing I have just described?"

Antonio looked around. He was pleased everyone had followed instructions.

"We will be working hard tomorrow," Antonio said. "And so tonight, we'll relax and enjoy a good meal cooked over a campfire."

Several older assistants appeared carrying driftwood logs and crates of food and water. Antonio and Rosario began working with some others carrying equipment, and soon they left the area.

"Alright!" Marisa yelled, with her hands in the air. "This is the life! Living on the beach. Sleeping under the stars. Cooking over an open fire. This is where I belong!"

Looking at her, Beto had to agree. Now that the sun was below the horizon and they were safely at their camp, she was barefoot and wore just her one-piece swimsuit and a pair of cargo shorts. Her long hair looked a little wild. Marisa looked exactly like she belonged here.

Beto made himself useful by helping to unpack the food. Dinner was going to be shish-kabobs cooked over the flames. The food looked delicious and he was very, very hungry.

Then he felt a large hand on his shoulder. He turned and found himself facing Antonio.

"Are you ready for your punishment, Beto?"

Antonio said.

Not knowing what else to say, Beto answered, "Yes, sir."

Antonio also grabbed Gonzalo and Juan. He herded all three boys to the campfire that was just starting to burn. Antonio's appearance commanded everyone's attention.

"One lesson you will learn from me is this," Antonio said to the group. "When you're living in nature, you can never entirely relax. There is always a threat. It might be a lightning storm. It might be a coyote. It might be losing your last liter of water because of a broken canteen. You must always be ready for the next threat, because nature will show you no mercy."

He paused to make sure they were fully paying attention. Every eye was on him and every ear was attuned.

"Tonight while you enjoy your meal, these students will supply the threat," Antonio said. "They will be three coyotes coming to steal your food. I am going to take them to the beach, where you can't see them. Their job is to get into our camp and ring that bell."

Antonio pointed to a metal pole just outside the campfire area. There was a little metal bell chained to it.

"That pole is where we hang our food so that animals don't get to it. When you hear that bell in the middle of the night, you had better wake up and make sure your food is safe. And tonight, if you hear that bell before you see one of these students, then three of you will be chosen for tomorrow night's challenge. So, if you want to sleep well tomorrow night, make sure you watch out for these boys tonight."

Antonio walked back to the beach with the three boys. At the beach, he led them north until they were out of sight of the camp.

"As soon as you ring that bell, you can come back to camp and sleep. If there is any food left, you can eat. Until then, here's a little jerky for each of you."

He handed them each a little chunk of hard, dry meat.

"If you do not ring that bell before sunrise, you'll be out here again tomorrow night."

Antonio turned to leave, then stopped.

"And watch out for snakes. We're in this area a lot, so they should be used to us. But you're going to be crawling through the grass. So be careful."

He walked down the beach and back towards the welcoming glow of the campfire over the dunes. The three boys exchanged worried glances.

"What now?" Gonzalo asked.

Beto tried to take a bite of his jerky. It was too hard to bite through.

"Let's think through this problem," Juan said. "First, they are all sitting in the light of the campfire. That's going to ruin their night vision. That's a good thing for us."

"But the bell is right there in the light," Gonzalo said.

"Yes, but at least it's on the edge of the camp," Juan said. "We should probably approach it from the dark side. What about our clothes?"

Beto was wearing a light colored shirt. That was not a good thing for sneaking around in the dark. Juan was wearing a black shirt. Gonzalo's was dark red.

"Okay, here's my plan," Juan said, kneeling on the ground. He drew a large 'X' in the sand. "That's the bell. We will slowly and quietly make our way inland. Then we'll split up as far apart as we can and slowly approach the camp from three different directions."

Juan drew this all in the sand.

"That's the plan?" Gonzalo asked.

"Beto, with your bright shirt, they'll see you first. Each time they see you, retreat and try again from a slightly different direction. You need to be a constant distraction. Gonzalo and I will try to be sneakier. Maybe we'll make it to the bell while they're focusing on you."

They trudged off into the high grass. Little bushes scratched their legs. Mosquitoes stung them. And worst of all, they could just barely hear the rest of the group over the dunes, enjoying a meal and having fun. Beto gnawed on his jerky, trying to get a small piece of it to break off as his stomach growled with hunger.

Juan led them forward. He had picked up a piece of driftwood, about the right size for a walking stick, and with this he prodded the ground in front of him, searching for snakes. Beto grabbed a similar stick as soon as he could find one.

Finally, in the midst of a vast, dark expanse of grass and waist-high shrubs, they stopped. The glow of the campfire was almost too faint to see.

"Okay, let's separate. And we'll just slowly move in. Beto, you don't need to be especially slow or careful. Just be seen every now and then."

Beto was left alone in the darkness. The stars were out and they shone with amazing clarity. He crouched down and began to slowly walk towards the campfire. His progress was slow. Thorns and branches snagged his shirt whenever he crouched too low.

He tried to follow little paths between the thickest parts of the scrub. He used a stick frequently to poke the ground in front of him. This caused some little animals to scurry away. He never saw what they were, but he was glad they ran away.

He worked his way up onto the top of a dune. From there he still could not see the fire. He would have to climb down the dune, across a low area, and up another dune. He picked up the pace down the dune and through this low area. He began to hear talking and laughing in the distance. By now, he thought, they were probably eating. Somebody else was sitting with Marisa and he was stuck out here in the hot, humid night with the mosquitoes and snakes.

How had he gotten into trouble? This time, it was Juan who had broken the windshield of the truck. Beto hadn't even known what Juan was up to. But just because they had submitted a project proposal together, Beto was in trouble again. His one hope was that somehow tonight someone would reach the bell so he wouldn't be stuck out here tomorrow night.

He began to climb upward again. By the time he reached the top of the dune, he was lying down in the sand. He could see into camp. And yes, everyone was having fun. A few people were still eating. Some guy was playing a guitar. A few girls were dancing around and singing. He recognized the song. "A Life Worth Living," by St. Max and the Fanatics. A classic his father used to sing when Beto was young.

It's time to be seen. He got up off the sand and began walking low, keeping as much of himself behind the low shrubs as he could. But the shrubs weren't even waist-high, so most of his torso was exposed.

He crept toward the fire and no one seemed to notice him. When the people in camp grew quiet, he laid down in the sand again. When the singing and dancing commenced, he snuck forward. He was probably within fifty meters of the camp when someone yelled out.

"Hey! There's one of the coyotes," the girl said. She pointed in his direction and the whole group waved at him. Beto waved back and walked away. Once over a sand dune, he circled towards the ocean and rested for a few minutes. He took another bite of the jerky and then he began his approach again. *This is going to be a long night.*

Beto went through this process three times, being seen quite easily each time. Only once did the group see one of the other boys, who weren't approaching as aggressively as Beto.

On the next approach, Beto just barely made it over the first sand dune when he was spotted. As he was turning away, he saw Antonio walking out in his direction. He stood still and waited.

As Antonio approached, he called out, "This is the worst attempt I've ever seen at moving stealthily. You're just going to exhaust yourself doing the same thing over and over. Use your head! Try something new!"

Beto realized Antonio was right. He really had no hope of not being seen.

"At least your two friends are being a little more sneaky than you," Antonio said. "If you don't start putting some effort into this, I can and will send you—"

The bell rang. Antonio froze.

"What the hell?" he said, as he turned and returned quickly back through the grass.

Beto followed. When they got back to the camp, Juan was standing by the pole smiling.

"How did he get in here and touch that bell?" Antonio demanded.

No one said a word.

"I had four people standing watch. Where are they?" Antonio said.

Three boys and a girl stood up.

"Did no one see him?" Antonio said. "Were you all asleep? I've been doing this for five years and no one has ever rung the bell this early. In fact, the only time the bell ever gets rung is if the sentries fall asleep late at night. You must be the stupidest and laziest group I've ever worked with!"

Antonio was really getting angry. He confronted one of the male sentries, a boy named Diego.

"You! Tell me how this coyote got to the bell while you were on your watch."

Diego was despondent. "He tricked me," he said.

"He tricked you?!" Antonio yelled. Veins were popping out of his neck and his face was turning red. He put his face inches away from Diego's. "How did he trick you?"

Diego squirmed, trying to avoid being so close to Antonio but knowing he could not move away.

"The guys who needed to go to the bathroom were going out that way," he said as he pointed in a roughly southwesterly direction. "Like you told us."

Antonio kept his face directly in front of Diego's face.

"And then this kid, Juan, comes walking back down the path looking like he had just gone to take a leak. I don't know him and I didn't remember who exactly was sent out to be a coyote."

"But you didn't see him leave the camp to take a leak?" Antonio said.

"I wasn't paying that close attention to who was leaving," Diego said. "I was a little suspicious when he walked into camp, but he didn't go to the bell. He walked over towards the campfire and sat down with everyone else."

"And no one noticed him?" Antonio yelled.

"And then a little while later, he just walked over to the bell and rang it," Diego said. "No one stopped him because we all saw him walk away from the fire to the bell."

Antonio was silent.

"That is freaking brilliant!" he finally said. "Juan, you genius, get over here!"

Juan jumped up and ran over to Antonio.

"I had planned to make you suffer much more than this," Antonio said, putting his arm around Juan's shoulder, "but you seem to have outsmarted this entire group of homeristas. You will all pay for this tomorrow."

With that, Antonio stomped off to his little command post near the bell pole. He sat down among the crates of supplies. "It's time to go to sleep now," he yelled over his shoulder. "I will be waking you up very early in the morning."

The group quietly prepared to sleep. The food was hung from the pole. The boys and girls separated onto different sides of the campfire. Gonzalo wandered back into camp and Beto quietly explained what had happened. And then Beto found a soft, clean spot in the sand and collapsed onto his back. As he watched the stars, he slowly drifted off to sleep.

Later in the night, someone grabbed his foot. He sat up and saw Marisa, holding her finger over her lips, signaling him to be quiet. She waved for him to follow her. She crawled through the sand and Beto followed. Once they were out of camp, she stood up and ran back towards the beach. Beto followed in the dark.

Marisa stopped and turned. When Beto approached, she kissed him on the cheek.

"You guys were brilliant," she whispered. "I've never seen Antonio so angry on the first night. You completely surprised him."

Beto nodded. He was kind of embarrassed that his part in this brilliant plot was just to be stupid and do the same thing over and over. And he had been good at it.

"We're going for a swim," Marisa said, pointing to the ocean.

"But what about getting up early in the morning like

Antonio said?" Beto asked.

"We might as well enjoy ourselves tonight," she answered. "Come on!"

Beto followed and saw several homeristas already in the calm waves. Marisa waded into the water up to her knees.

"It was so hot by the fire," she said. "It feels great to cool off."

Beto stepped tentatively into the water as well. Marisa's eyes focused on his foot.

"Is your prosthesis going to be okay in the saltwater?" she asked.

Beto nodded. "It should be okay. I've been swimming with it before. The salt and sand probably won't be good for it long term, but it's not like I can avoid sand and saltwater out here."

"You can't lose it in the water, can you?"

Beto shook his head. "The base is permanently anchored in bone. The rest screws on and then locks it in place. It's not going anywhere."

"Oh, okay," Marissa said.

"We're supposed to always go into the water in pairs," she said, "For safety. So you can be my pair for tonight. If a shark bites me, it's your job to drag me back to shore."

Beto hoped she was joking.

She executed a shallow dive into the next wave. Beto followed and tried to stay close. Marisa swam away from the beach. Beto was glad he was a good swimmer because he had no idea where she was going or how long she planned to stay in the water. But it was worth the uncertainty and the danger to be this close to her, and to know he was the one guy she had chosen to share this midnight swim with.

Marisa continued to swim away from shore. After a while she floated on her back and looked at the stars. Beto thought it was interesting that she just assumed he would follow her wherever she went, whatever she did.

"There's the north star," she said. "And there's Cassiopeia just over it. Cassiopeia was supposed to be one of the most beautiful women to have ever lived. But she was too proud, so she was banished to the sky and her throne spins around the north star forever. For half of all eternity, she is upside down in the sky."

"That's a harsh punishment for being proud," Beto said.

"But it's a good lesson. It's okay to be awesome, but don't brag about it too much, or people will make you suffer for it."

Marisa swam a little farther and then stood up.

"Sand bar!" she said.

Beto found his footing and stood up as well.

"Beto, I wanted to tell you something."

Beto suddenly felt guilty for being out here alone with Marisa. She was beautiful and athletic and fun and perfect in every way, but Beto kept thinking that Adriana would be jealous. Which was ridiculous. He and Adriana were just friends.

"I keep expecting you to make a move on me, Beto. And then I was planning to tell you that I really just want to be friends. I like you a lot. But you haven't made your move, so I can't turn you away," Marisa said.

Beto tried to sort through this complicated explanation.

"I was trying to be polite," Beto said. "I think it's great for guys and girls to be friends, without one of them having to worry about the other one wanting to get romantic."

In his mind, Beto truly believed what he had just said. But there was something deep in his body that told him he was lying.

"That's exactly what I think," Marisa smiled. "But all the guys I know always want to start getting all physical. I like guys a lot. But I just want a friend."

"I can be that!" Beto said.

Marisa sat on the sand bar and the water came up to her neck.

"Besides," she said, "I think Adriana is depending on you to be with her."

"You think so?" Beto asked.

"Everyone who knows her thinks so," Marisa laughed. "You two are the perfect couple. You're both smart and nice and interesting. Everyone likes you."

Beto sat down next to Marisa. He felt oddly good about this. True, he was on the sand bar with the wrong girl, but at least someone had clearly told him who the right girl was. He wished life could always be this easy.

Chapter 15 - The Hunt Begins

In which Beto and the homeristas learn to hunt for food and government agents intrude into this experimental utopia.

Beto was awakened by a boy he hardly knew, but he knew his name was Luis. It was still dark. Luis signaled for Beto to follow him. Beto followed and saw the entire camp gathering at the fire circle. Everyone was silent. When everyone had gathered, Antonio quietly addressed the group.

"We are going to quickly and silently move our entire camp to a new location. We are going to do this now and be gone long before dawn. I want every bit of evidence that we were here removed. Do it now."

The entire group scattered. Since they had so little gear and since the leaders had made sure all the group gear had been put in order the night before, it took almost no time for the group to be ready to leave. Beto noticed Luis and another boy sweeping the sand with branches from one of the little shrubs. There would not even be footprints left behind.

Antonio led them inland along a narrow path. They walked single file. Beto stumbled along, half asleep. His artificial foot made him feel clumsy and loud. There was a slight red glow in the east when Antonio stopped. They were in a flat area that looked exactly like every other place they had walked, except there was a pile of supplies that students began to unstack and organize.

"These crates contain your morning meal. You have five minutes to eat and finish all of the water you brought with you. Afterwards, refill all your canteens. Do this all silently."

Once again, everyone moved. It looked like chaos, but they were accomplishing exactly what they had been told.

Beto walked over to the supplies and someone handed him an apple and an unwrapped nutrition bar. *Breakfast!*

"Eat everything, except the seeds. Then keep the seeds in your pocket," said the girl who handed him the food.

After just a few minutes, Antonio began to separate the mass of students into smaller groups. Beto, Gonzalo, and Juan were put in a group with two other students, a boy named Ed and a girl named Alex. It was quite bright now and the sun was just about to rise above the horizon.

Antonio addressed the group.

"Welcome to the field lab. Everything we do in the next two days has one goal—to teach you how to survive in the natural world in a way that actually benefits the natural world. We have had students living in these desert regions of south Texas for five years now, learning how we can best live here. Over that time we have carefully studied our impact on this very delicate and slow-growing ecosystem.

"Today, we have three goals. One group will continue their work of restoring the native grassland in order to increase the native animal diversity. That's a nice way of saying they will be cutting down invasive trees and brush. Someday soon, this grassland will be ready for hunting.

"The second group will practice some very basic fishing techniques using spears and nets they have made by hand. This fishing is licensed by the state parks and wildlife department and it meets our own, even higher, standards of sustainability. If they are successful, we will eat well tonight. If not, we will go hungry."

There were shouts of encouragement for the fishers.

"And finally," he said, looking towards Beto's group, "we have a group of future hunters who will be practicing. They will help us learn to survive in our many inland sites.

"Work hard today. The things you learn may be the hope of humanity's future."

They're counting on me to be the hope of humanity's future? Beto wondered. *That's a lot of pressure.*

Antonio approached Beto's group.

"You've all seen how well our archers have learned to make and use bows and arrows. The small game we hunt in the desert is crucial for the group's ability to survive. We know we can do this with bows. However, Juan has put together a proposal for using a simpler weapon. His little group will be trying to use slings for hunting.

"I'm not sure if this is a good idea or not, but the

purpose of the field lab is to try new things. You three will have a chance this year to prove or disprove the usefulness of slings."

That sounded fair to Beto.

"Here's what we're going to do. We're going to set up bird-sized targets at a distance of twenty meters. Each of you will stay here until you hit your target one hundred times. When you reach that number, *if* you reach that number, come to me and I'll send you out on a hunt. You can help provide food for tonight.

"I'm confident our archers will be able to do this. You slingers… this will be your chance to practice. You will eat lunch after you hit the first fifty targets. Any questions?"

What if we don't hit fifty targets? Does that mean no lunch?

No one had any questions they were willing to pose to Antonio, so they began to set up their targets. The two bow and arrow users had no problem hitting their targets. Most of their time was spent leisurely retrieving their arrows. It was obvious they would make their lunchtime goal.

The slingers had a very different experience. Of the three of them, only Juan had ever practiced before. He was able to get his rocks to go in approximately the right direction. Beto and Gonzalo threw their rocks in wildly unpredictable directions.

It soon became obvious they were facing another unanticipated problem. Whereas arrows were easy to find after they missed their mark, rocks were not. And this sandy landscape had no rocks at all to use for additional ammunition. The supply of small roundish rocks Juan had brought with him quickly dwindled.

An hour into their practice session, they were out of rocks and had not hit a single target.

"This is discouraging," Gonzalo said, as he sat down to take a rest. "My whole body is sore. I didn't think it would be easy, but I didn't think it would be this hard either."

"We need more ammo," Juan said. "We have lots of seashells. I don't think they'll fly straight, though."

They had no choice—broken seashells were all they had. It was well before noon when the archers had finished all one hundred of their hits. They tried the slings as well, but had little luck with them. By noon, the three boys had hit targets a few times each, mainly due to luck.

Alex and Ed left to eat lunch and then go out to hunt. Alex made a mild attempt to stay behind with the slingers, but Juan told her it was okay to go. The bows and arrows had proved their effectiveness and it was time for them to be used in the hunt.

All through the long, hot afternoon Juan, Gonzalo, and Beto continued to work on their technique. Realizing this was their fate for the day, they took their time and thought about how they would have to do this in a hunting situation. There would be no time for a big windup. Each throw would have to be quick and silent.

By the time evening came, they were each pretty confident that they could execute a clean release of whatever was in the sling. It was impossible to predict what the curvy shells would do once released, but they imagined with nice, round rocks they would have a pretty good chance of hitting a large target. Hitting a small bird about to take flight still seemed unlikely.

Just after sunset they were called in to dinner, which consisted of a variety of fish and crabs, along with potatoes and native roots that had been baked in the coals of the big campfire. Beto was exhausted, but he had survived. Antonio had even stopped yelling at him .

When dinner was finished, Beto fell asleep in the sand. People around him were telling stories and singing songs as he drifted into sleep, glad to be with this amazing group of people.

The next morning, Beto awoke to noise and confusion. There were harsh voices having some sort of discussion he couldn't quite understand. Then Antonio's voice awoke everyone.

"Wake up, people!" he said. "I need everyone to gather around me right now."

Beto stood up and stretched his muscles. He had slept well. He stumbled towards Antonio's voice in the predawn light.

He was surprised to see the two border patrol officers, Noriega and Clemente, standing with Antonio. When all the students had gathered, Antonio spoke again.

"These officers want to make sure we have no undocumented people with us today," Antonio said. "Please make a line and give them your names. The school will be able to verify who you all are. There's no need to worry. They say this is just a routine check."

The students did as they were told. All of their names

were recorded. Then Officer Clemente looked around the camp. When she saw the fish bones near the fire, she asked to see fishing licenses. Antonio was able to show her what she wanted to see. But even after that, she paced around the camp, looking suspiciously at everything.

"How many of these campsites do you have?" she asked Antonio.

"We have this site for training. And then we have at least one at each ranch where we do research and brush clearing. I'd guess we have made dozens of them over the years. Why do you ask?"

Officer Clemente shook her head. "Research?" she said. "Can't you find someplace nicer than this desert to do your work?"

"This is the ecosystem that surrounds our school," Antonio explained. "We study the natural world as part of our hands-on curriculum."

Clemente still looked suspicious. "I'm ready," she said to Noriega. "Let's go."

The two border patrol officers got into the four-wheel drive electro-cart and drove away.

"What were they looking for?" Rosario asked Antonio.

"Who knows? I guess anything that would make the school look bad. I'll bet Dr. Cruz's mining company called them to complain about us. If they can get the school out of the way, then the mining company will be free to do whatever it wants."

The students ate a simple breakfast. Marisa ate with Beto.

"It's *unbelievable* that we come out here in the middle of nowhere to do our outdoor research," Marisa said, "and even way out *here* the government and industry harass us. It's like it's not enough that they have every city filled with people and pollution, they always want more."

Beto thought about this. It was odd, he thought, that there was no way people could simply escape other people.

Rosario had overheard Marisa and she came and sat down, eating her NutriVitaPro bar.

"You know, *people* are the most vicious predators the world has ever seen, in terms of outright destruction. We *outlast* and *out-reproduce* any other large species on earth. You can *kill* one of us, or an entire village, but in a generation all those empty spaces will be filled with more people hungry for more resources. We survive by killing and eating other creatures. We are like the nightmare species we write sci-fi about."

"But not us, right?" Beto said. "I mean, aren't we out here to learn how to live in nature without destroying it?"

"We're trying to move in that direction," Marisa said. "But it's hard. Look at this NutriVitaPro bar. In order to grow the plants and animals we need to make these vitamins and minerals, we have to clear giant areas of native ecosystems. We just wipe out everything native and replace it with miles and miles of the crops and herds we want."

Beto hadn't thought about that before. His eyes were being opened to a lot of things.

The students spent the rest of the day clearing brush

so that native grass would be able to return. And with the grass would come quail and turkeys and many other species. This one little area will be made better by humans, rather than destroyed by them, Rosario said.

The foreign students, which included most of the students present, were still upset and scared by the aggressive tactics the border patrol had used. But as they did their work, their fears subsided.

Chapter 16 - Seeds in the Desert

In which preparations for a lifetime are made.

"See where the soil is still wet from the flood last week? That's where we're going to plant these seeds," the woman said.

The man nodded and began to make small holes in the moist soil. He dropped one bean in each hole.

"You think these will survive out here?" the man asked.

"Most won't, but some will," the woman said. "And we aren't even planting most of them. We're stashing enough bags to last a lifetime if someone takes care of them."

"What if the border patrol finds these caches?" the man asked. "They have dogs that can track people. It won't be hard to find this place if they look."

"What will they find? Seeds. Beans. Maybe a few snares for hunting. They have many other problems to chase in the desert. I don't think we'll be a high priority."

Chapter 17 - Ghosts

In which a tropical storm approaches, a secret is discovered beneath the school, and hints of the woman in white are detected again.

As Beto and Marisa kayaked back across the channel, Beto couldn't believe he had only been away from the school for two days. It seemed like a month. So much had happened. He had made new friends. His friendship with Marisa and Gonzalo and Juan had deepened. He was proud of the number of challenges he had overcome.

He was even reluctant to turn his neuro chip back on. It seemed to intrude on the peaceful sense of self-reliance and confidence he had discovered over the last two days. A dozen unimportant messages flooded his mind as the neuro net reconnected to his brain. Beto ignored them all, deleting them without taking the time to listen to even one of them. He wanted to regain the silence that he had discovered.

When the kayaks landed on the shore of the island, Beto felt like he was a returning hero. He had been one of only a few sophomores who had been accepted into the field lab program, and he had done well. Antonio had stopped being mean to him as soon as it became clear that Beto's skills in fish cleaning were the best of anyone in the program. And once Beto was on Antonio's good side, so were Gonzalo and Juan.

Beto and Marisa lifted up their kayak and were carrying it to the storage shed when Beto saw Adriana sitting on a sand dune. She waved. He tried to wave back, but one hand held the back of the kayak and the other was full of gear.

They stowed the kayak on its wooden shelf and closeted the paddles and PFDs. As they left the shed, Marisa gave Beto a friendly one-armed hug and then headed to the girls' dorm. Adriana was still waiting, so Beto was glad Marisa's good-bye had been quick and not too affectionate.

"How was it?" Adriana asked as Beto walked over to her.

"Tiring, but great!" Beto said. "What are you waiting out here for?"

"I knew you were coming back this evening, so I did my English homework out here. I watched the kayaks come all the way across the water."

Beto sat next to her. Gonzalo and Juan saw them together and walked quickly past. Beto was very nervous. He knew he should say something, but he wasn't sure what that thing was. He decided to fall back on his manners, and to simply be polite and honest.

"Thanks for waiting for me," Beto said. "I thought about you a lot while we were out there."

"You did?" Adriana said. "The other girls didn't distract you?"

"Well, there are other girls, and there's you," Beto said. "You are in a different category."

Adriana moved slightly closer and took Beto's hand. He had said the right thing.

The next day it was back to class. The day started with morning chapel. It seemed very early as Beto stumbled into a pew near the front. Adriana found him and sat next to him.

Sister Elizondo, dressed in her standard Franciscan brown robe, stood at the lectern in the center of the dimly lit chapel. She began to read.

"When some were speaking about the temple, how it was adorned with beautiful stones and gifts dedicated to God, he said, 'As for these things that you see, the days will come when not one stone will be left upon another; all will be thrown down.'

"They asked him, 'Teacher, when will this be, and what will be the sign that this is about to take place?' And he said, 'Beware that you are not led astray; for many will come in my name and say, "I am he!" and, "The time is near!" Do not go after them.

"'When you hear of wars and insurrections, do not be terrified; for these things must take place first, but the end will not follow immediately.' Then he said to them, 'Nation will rise against nation, and kingdom against kingdom; there will be great earthquakes, and in various places famines and plagues; and there will be dreadful portents and great signs from heaven.'"

Well, that's a very dark and depressing thought to

start the day, Beto thought.

Sister Elizondo continued.

"'But before all this occurs, they will arrest you and persecute you; they will hand you over to synagogues and prisons, and you will be brought before kings and governors because of my name. This will give you an opportunity to testify. So make up your minds not to prepare your defense in advance; for I will give you words and a wisdom that none of your opponents will be able to withstand or contradict. You will be betrayed even by parents and brothers, by relatives and friends; and they will put some of you to death. You will be hated by all because of my name. But not a hair of your head will perish. By your endurance you will gain your souls.'"

"I definitely don't understand that," Beto whispered to Adriana.

Adriana thought for a moment, then in her heavy accent, she whispered back.

"Good people trying to do good things are still going to suffer. It's just the way the world is. But it is still worth it to do good."

Sister Elizondo gave Adriana an annoyed look. Then, when silence once again fell over the chapel, she prayed.

"God, Giver of Life, help us to cherish the time we have. Help us to care for the people we can touch. Help us to see light through the darkness. Amen."

As the students got up to leave, Gonzalo walked up beside Beto.

"Do you believe in all that end of the world stuff?"

Gonzalo said.

"I guess the world has to end sometime," Beto said.

"Yeah, but Juan says people probably won't even still be here billions of years from now when all that happens," Gonzalo said.

Adriana jumped into the conversation.

"I don't think this morning's reading was talking about the physical end of the world. I think it was talking more about the giant catastrophes that happen in all of our lives. Everyone has to face big, scary things. In fact, I think all those things in today's reading have already happened a long time ago."

"But Jesus hasn't come back yet," Gonzalo said. "Isn't that what Sister Elizondo was talking about?"

"Maybe he's always coming back," Adriana said. "Maybe the way we face every crisis shows who we really are and what we really believe."

"You could be right," Beto said. "There are wars and earthquakes and famines going on right now."

"Yeah, but I was always told there was going to be one big ending and then Jesus would come and take over," Gonzalo said.

The rush to get to class brought the conversation to an end. But Beto continued to think of wars and earthquakes and famine.

Ms. Lin had written a new saying from Confucius for the week: "When the master went inside the Great Temple he asked questions about everything. Someone said, How can it be said that the son of Zhou understands the rites when he asks questions about everything? When the master heard this he said, The asking of questions is in itself the correct rite (Analects 3.15)."

Ms. Lin stood in front of the class calmly waiting for everyone to get in their seats and settle down. Beto noticed that without saying a word she always managed to quiet the entire class.

"Students think that learning is about learning the answers," Ms. Lin said. "It is not. You will never find all the answers. But the correct questions will lead you closer and closer to the right path. For now, you have good teachers to ask the right questions for you. But someday, you must know how to ask the right questions yourselves."

"What is she talking about?" the Voice said. "World history with Ms. Lin is like unraveling an endless set of riddles."

Adriana rolled her eyes. "Is she as clueless in the field lab as she is in class?" she asked Beto.

Beto shook his head. "No. She's a natural in the field lab. Out there she fits right in. She does everything great once she's out of the classroom."

"Mr. Gonzalez?" It was Ms. Lin's voice. "Do you have something to add to today's lesson?"

"Yes, Ms. Lin," Beto said, knowing this was the best answer to give, although since he hadn't been paying attention it was not entirely true. He looked at the board.

"The asking of questions is in itself the correct rite," Beto read from the board. He was stalling. Then, a brilliant idea came to him. "All of us are being asked questions by our visiting professor, Dr. Esquivel. She has a Ph.D., but she is here asking questions of high school students."

"Way to go, Beto!" the Voice said. "Answer her with mysterious riddles."

Ms. Lin waited for Beto to continue.

"Maybe it is because she knows so much, that she knows how important it is to learn from us."

Ms. Lin smiled. "Very good, Mr. Gonzalez. Does anyone else have anything to add to that?"

Marisa raised her hand. Ms. Lin called on her.

"What do you, as a teacher, think of Dr. Esquivel's project?" Marisa asked.

"I think it will be interesting to hear her results, as someone from outside the school," Ms. Lin replied.

"What does it matter what her results say?" Marisa asked.

Ms. Lin smiled. "Tell me. If I were to mention the names George Washington and King George III of England, which of these men would you say you had generally positive regards for, and which do you have generally negative regards for?"

"Obviously, George Washington is the good guy and King George was the bad guy. We learn that in U.S. history," Marisa answered.

"Exactly. You do not learn just the facts. You learn who was good and who was bad—who was the hero for your country and who was the enemy. Do you think British citizens think the same of King George III as Americans do?"

"Probably not," Marisa admitted.

"This is why Dr. Esquivel's answers will be

interesting. The heroes and the villains in this school's story will soon be named."

"What if we disagree with her interpretation?" Marisa asked.

"You may. But one way or another, some version of this school's history is about to be written. Students twenty years from now will form their opinions based on the story we agree upon."

"That's scary," Marisa said.

"It is a heavy responsibility," Ms. Lin said.

From that point on, the Voice began a preemptive attempt to establish the accepted history of the school. "Are we going to accept it when we're told *Director Contreras* is the heroic leader of this school? Or are we going to *tell the truth*—that he's moody and arbitrary—that he is *obsessed* with the ghost of his wife. And what about Antonio? Is he a *bully* or a *hero*? We, the students, must decide. Don't let the *authorities* tell you what to think."

The Voice was so energized by this campaign to control the opinion of the student body that Adriana finally got sick of hearing it and stopped listening. Beto could tell Adriana was aggravated with him for continuing to listen, but everyone was talking about it. As a new student, he didn't want to be left out of the conversation.

Cleaning the third floor hallway, he learned that the students were not the only ones worried about the results of Dr. Esquivel's mythology. Beto stumbled upon a heated discussion between Director Contreras and Dr. Esquivel.

"International flavor and strong academics! Is that all you've found in all the conversations you've had with our students?" the director said. "That sounds like an advertisement for the old school. We are much different from that."

"That's not what your students think," Dr. Esquivel said. "I'm only reporting what they told me."

"Then you must visit the field lab. They will show you another vision."

"I don't think I have the time to do that, Justo," Dr. Esquivel said.

"I cannot accept any other answer. You must go. Or you cannot hope to understand this school."

Dr. Esquivel sounded exasperated. "Let me think about it, Justo."

"Excellent. Think about it. We will find a way to get you out there and talk to the students in that environment."

"Alright, but I am running out of time. I need to get back to my research and students at the university. We didn't plan on this taking as long as it has."

"Tell me what you need. I'll transport you back and forth. I'll do whatever it takes for you to hear the rest of the story."

"I'll let you know what my department head says," Dr. Esquivel said.

Beto kept his head down and started mopping again as Dr. Esquivel quickly exited the office. She paid no attention to him at all.

Beto reported this story to Adriana, Gonzalo, and Juan at dinner.

"Everyone is upset about this!" Adriana said. "Why can't we just focus on being a good school? Why do we have to worry about writing a mythology for ourselves? How is that going to help me get into a good college or get a good job? Listening to what all the students think—it's just a bunch of stories."

"Speaking of stories," Gonzalo said. "I overheard some seniors talking about the underground chambers below the school."

"What did they say is down there?" Beto asked.

"No one knows. But they think it has something to do with the time this building was owned by the military. In World War II, prisoners were held here. And there's a ghost here as well."

"A ghost?" Beto said, remembering the odd experience he had during his first week at the school.

"The woman in white," Gonzalo said.

Those words stunned Beto.

"What's wrong?" Adriana asked.

"It's true. I've seen the woman in white," Beto said.

Beto's claim made Gonzalo insist that they search for an entrance into the underground chambers again.

"I can't believe you didn't tell me you saw the ghost," Gonzalo said.

"I didn't see a ghost. I saw a woman in white," Beto insisted.

The four friends made a plan to meet on the first floor of the classroom building at midnight. Beto went to the library to get as much homework done as possible before the night's adventures began. It was there that Marisa walked up to him with a sense of urgency.

"Have you heard the news?" she said.

"No, I'm trying to study. I have all the channels on my neuro chip turned off," he said.

"Get back on. There's a big tropical storm entering the gulf."

"What does that mean?"

"Look at the map. In three days it will be here. We'll be evacuating. Parents are already driving up from Mexico to pick up their kids."

"How long will the evacuation last?" Beto asked, as he studied the map on his neuro chip.

"How long until we can have classes in a flooded building? Sea level has risen several feet since the last hurricane hit here. Four days from now, this building may not even exist."

That was the end of Beto's productive study time. He spent the rest of the evening worrying about what would happen if the school were destroyed. The hours until midnight slowly dragged by. After 'lights out' at ten thirty, he lay in his bed and stared at the crack in his bedroom's ceiling.

At midnight, dressed in his darkest clothes, Beto snuck down to the plaza. Gonzalo and Juan were already there. Gonzalo had thought to bring two flashlights. Adriana walked onto the plaza, and as soon as she saw Beto she ran to him and hugged him.

"I'm leaving tomorrow," she said.

Beto held onto her, wondering what the future held for them.

"Okay, we're all leaving tomorrow," Juan said

impatiently. "So let's solve this mystery tonight."

He led them through the shadows to the academic building. He opened the door with the key and walked to the stairway going up. He pulled out a small bag and began dusting the stairs with a powder.

"Flour," he said. "If the woman in white leaves footsteps, then she's not a ghost."

Juan did the same on the first few steps of every stairway. Then he led them back onto the plaza, locking the doors behind them, and led them over to one of the auditorium exits. It opened when he pulled on it.

"Why is that open?" Gonzalo asked.

"After our last fiasco, I've been working on the lock," Juan said. "I don't want to get caught hanging out of a window again."

"And where did you get the key to the academic building?" Adriana asked.

Juan smiled. "I'm the leader of the floor cleaning team. If I don't have a key, the floors don't get clean."

Juan led them into the auditorium. It was dark, but there was a little bit of light coming in from the plaza. Beto felt his way slowly up the aisle, touching each row of seats. Adriana held onto his belt. The floor slowly rose as they worked their way to the back of the huge room.

When they opened the door into the foyer, it was pitch black. Only then did Gonzalo dare to turn on a flashlight. The foyer had one wall of doors that entered into the auditorium, and one wall of doors that entered into the second floor of the classroom building. On opposite sides of the room, two stairways led up to the balcony. Beneath each stairway was a restroom.

Juan led the group to a door outside the girls' restroom.

"Students go into the restrooms all the time, so we know we probably won't find anything there," he said. "But this door is locked with a deadbolt."

"It's probably full of cleaning supplies," Beto said.

"Probably," Juan said. "It's also underneath the stairs. If there is a stairway down, this would be a good place for it."

"So, how do we get in?" Gonzalo asked.

Juan pointed to the exposed hinges. He took off the backpack he had slung on his back, pulled out a screwdriver and hammer, and began working to pull the pins out of the hinges. Each pin took a few hard blows from the hammer, but he was quick about it. They listened to see if they could hear any noise coming from the hallway that would indicate Mr. Silva was coming to investigate. All was silent.

Juan pried the door off the hinges and they squeezed into the dark room. Metal shelves with cleaning supplies lined the walls. But it was a larger room than they had expected. And on the far side of the room, on the floor, was a metal hatch.

"We've found it!" Gonzalo exclaimed.

Unfortunately, the metal door was padlocked. They could lift it about an inch, but even when they shone a flashlight in, they could see nothing.

"So, I guess we can assume they're not housing undocumented people here," Juan said.

"Was that one of the theories?" Adriana asked.

Juan nodded.

"What about old supplies that nobody cares about anymore?" Beto asked.

"That's not a very interesting theory," Gonzalo said.

"How old would you say this lock is?" Juan asked. "This is the first year of our school's operation. The lock is definitely older than that."

"What about the previous school? How long was it here?"

No one knew.

"I guess this is a dead end," Beto said.

"Unless we want to risk breaking the lock," Juan said. "If Mr. Silva has never used this lock, we could break it and he might never notice."

"And if he does?" Adriana asked.

"Then we're in trouble again," Juan said.

"If he does use the lock, then the combination is probably written down somewhere," Gonzalo said.

"But where? How would we ever find it?" Adriana asked.

"We might never find it, true. But it could be right around here somewhere." Gonzalo said. "Let's look around."

It took them only a few minutes to find three numbers written in permanent marker on one of the metal shelves. Juan tried the numbers on the rusty lock and it reluctantly opened. He swung open the metal door. A spiral staircase led down into the darkness.

"Now what?" Adriana said. "Is someone really going to go down there?"

"Someone?" Juan said. "We've all got to go down."

"Why?" Adriana asked.

"Because this is our adventure. This is our last day before we have to leave and we might never come back."

Juan led the way. The metal stairway was rusted and dusty. The flashlight was too weak to illuminate much beyond the staircase itself. The four of them slowly wound their way down the staircase. There was a strong smell of something moldy and rotten.

"I'm at the bottom," Juan said. "It's kind of wet down here."

Beto reached the bottom. Adriana was holding onto him. The floor was concrete. The smell was even stronger.

"Let's stay together," Adriana said. "I don't want anybody wandering off and disappearing."

"How dangerous can it be?" Juan said. "Nobody can be down here, with the door locked the way it was."

"Unless there's another way in," Beto said.

"Okay, we'll stay close together," Juan agreed.

"Let's follow the wall around," Gonzalo said.

Juan started walking with his left hand on the wall. He encountered a large wooden work table. Pieces of old equipment were randomly laid on the table.

"What is this stuff?" Gonzalo asked. "It looks like old electronics."

"Computers," Juan said. "From when they used to be big clunky things outside of our bodies instead of small internal devices."

"Let's keep going," Beto said.

Juan continued. He came to one corner of the room

and continued down the next wall. Several benches lined the wall. Beyond the benches he encountered a caged enclosure. It had a door chained shut with a padlock on the chain. Juan jiggled the chain. It was locked. Their flashlights revealed more old and dusty junk inside the cage.

"Wait!" Adriana said. "I heard a noise upstairs. Did we leave the closet door open?"

"If someone closes that metal hatch and locks it, we could be in big trouble. They might never find us down here," Beto said.

"But what if it's Mr. Silva..." Gonzalo said.

"I'd rather get in trouble than be locked down here," Beto said, as he ran back to the staircase.

Adriana was right by his side. They hurried up the spiral staircase. Beto poked his head through the hatchway. No lights were on and he heard no noise. He and Adriana climbed back up into the cleaning closet. The door to the foyer was closed. They heard no noises and saw no lights. They were about to turn around when Gonzalo ran into him. Beto heard the hatch door close. Juan was locking the lock.

"What happened?" Adriana said.

"Let's get out of here, fast," Gonzalo said. He ran into the foyer and kept going. Juan was right behind him. Beto and Adriana followed and finally caught up to them in the auditorium.

"What did you find down there?" Adriana asked.

"There was a body," Juan said. "An old, dead body."

"Where?" Beto asked.

"We found a repair pit where mechanics can work beneath cars," Gonzalo said. "On the side of the pit were some rusty metal doors we assumed were for tool storage. Most of them were empty. But I swear I saw an old body in one of them."

Beto would have suspected Gonzalo was joking, but his face showed that he was seriously scared.

"An old body?" Adriana said. "What did it look like?

"I just saw it for a second when Juan opened the metal door," Gonzalo said. "When Juan took off running, I ran too."

"This is crazy," Adriana said. "Why would there be a body in the basement of the school?"

"What kind of person was it?" Beto asked. "What did it look like?"

"It was an old guy," Juan said. "With old clothes."

"Are you sure he was dead?" Beto said.

"He was like a skeleton," Juan said. "There wasn't much skin."

"Let's get out of here," Gonzalo said.

They quietly made their way back across the plaza.

"Wait," Adriana said. "The hinges on the door. We've got to put the door back, or Mr. Silva will know someone's been down there."

No one wanted to go back. Finally, Beto agreed to go. Adriana reluctantly offered to go with him, but he refused.

"If someone's going to get in trouble, it's better if it's just one of us," he said.

Beto walked back into the auditorium and up the dark aisle. Once in the foyer, he lifted the loose door and realized getting it back on its hinges was going to be harder than he thought. It took a lot of balancing and shoving, but he finally got the pins back in the hinges.

Relieved that he had finally finished the job, he sat on the carpet with his back to the door. It was then that he saw a dim light beneath the doors that led to the classroom building. The light moved down the hall, but he heard no footsteps. *It's the ghost again!* he thought. He had to get a closer look.

He quickly ran out of the foyer and down the auditorium aisle. He exited the auditorium, crossed the plaza, and looked up to the second floor of the classroom building. He saw nothing. He tried the first floor doors, but they were all locked. There was no way in!

But then he realized the foyer doors had to open from the inside. He could have gone straight into the classroom building if he had thought of that. So he ran back in the auditorium, up the aisle, and into the dark foyer. He looked beneath the doors, but saw no light. Quietly, he opened a door. All that he saw was a dark hallway. He stepped into the hallway and closed the door behind him. As it clicked shut, he realized he was locked out of the foyer. He tried the door, just in case he needed a quick exit. It was indeed locked.

The only way out now was along the great hallway and then down the stairs to the first floor. Whatever was making the light, he hoped it wasn't dangerous. The stone carvings on the top of each column along the wall took on strange forms in the shadows. Being alone in the dark in the huge hallway was disconcerting, so he stayed close to one wall.

He walked as quietly as he could, his foot clicking against the floor. He wondered what the light had been and where it had gone. It couldn't have been Mr. Silva. His keys always jingled and his boots clumped noisily wherever he went.

Beto walked down the hall and looked into each open classroom. He saw nothing unusual and heard no noise. After searching the second floor, he thought about whether to go up or down. He remembered the woman in white looking out the first floor window. The thought sent a chill down his spine, but he knew he had to look downstairs.

He crept down the stairs. There was no ghostly woman looking out the door at the bottom of the stairs. He looked into the dark first floor hallway. Again, there was nothing unusual to be seen. There were two more exit doors to check. Thinking that the woman in white could be near made it difficult to move forward. Fear was building up in him and he almost could not move.

Then he heard a noise from upstairs. It had sounded as if a desk had been moved. He ran up the stairs and into the great hallway. He looked down the hall and saw a dim flicker of light. As he looked at it, it disappeared. He ran toward it. It had been near the last classroom on the side of the building nearest the boys' dorm—Ms. Lin's classroom. When he reached the classroom, he could see nothing but desks and chairs.

He sniffed the air. There was the faint smell of something sweet. He walked into the room and the smell was gone. The saying of Confucius was still on the board.

He touched the black letters, leaving a white streak as his fingers erased the ink where his finger touched. He just wanted some physical proof that all of the weird stuff happening was real.

He walked back into the hall; there was no smell. He was at a loss. He stood with his back against the wall in the great hallway and stared into the darkness.

Not knowing what else to do, he walked downstairs, out the door and returned to the dorm. The outdoors smelled like the sea. The dorm smelled like dirty socks. What had the smell near Ms. Lin's classroom been?

He walked into his dorm room, ready to collapse. But a dark form grabbed him.

"What took so long?" It was Gonzalo. He and Juan had been waiting in Beto's room.

Beto told them the whole story—how hard it had been to get the door back in place and then seeing the light and detecting the faint sweet scent. Gonzalo and Juan were entranced by the ghost story.

"So, you've seen her at the middle glass door of the first floor and Ms. Lin's classroom," Juan said. "What do those two places have in common?"

Beto shrugged. Juan suddenly jumped from his bed and ran for the door.

"Where are you going?" Gonzalo asked.

Then Beto remembered the flour Juan had dusted the stairs with.

"He's going to see if the woman in white left footprints," Beto said.

All three boys quickly and quietly hurried back to

the academic building.

In the central stairway Juan found a perfect footprint. Even in the dim light of his flashlight, a small, bare footprint could be seen.

"I can't believe it," Gonzalo said quietly. "She's real."

"It's so small," Beto said. "Is she a child?"

Juan looked for other footprints or any other sign that someone had been here.

"You said you smelled a sweet smell," Juan said.

"Not here," Beto answered, "but up in Ms. Lin's classroom."

The boys found nothing else on the stairway and detected no scent in or around Ms. Lin's classroom. Beto's smudge on Ms. Lin's writing was still there. They finally gave up searching for the night and went to their dorm rooms. The three boys fell asleep trying to decode the riddle of the woman in white.

Chapter 18 - The Storm Comes

In which preparations are made for the hurricane and a surprise visit from the Border Patrol upsets many people in the school.

Breakfast was chaos the next morning. The tropical storm was now a hurricane and the announcement had been made that the school was going to be evacuated. Students whose families lived within three hundred miles were going to be sent home. The rest would be put on a train and taken inland where they would sleep on the gym floors of local schools and churches.

Beto's family lived right at the point where they could choose whether to pick him up or let him go on the train. Although his mother was very worried about him and wanted to come and get him, Beto chose to go with the other students on the train. He knew his parents would have a hard time affording an electrocar rental for that distance, especially since prices had skyrocketed due to the hurricane. If he went home now, he wouldn't be able to afford to go home for Christmas.

Every student in the dining hall was having similar

conversations with their parents and friends. Adriana was going home, as were Gonzalo and Juan.

"What if we never come back?" Adriana said. "What if there's too much damage to the school for us to return?"

"This building's been here for eighty years," Gonzalo said. "It's survived lots of storms like this."

Juan didn't care much about the hurricane. He was still upset about the body he had seen.

"Who do we tell about the dead man in the basement?" he said. "We shouldn't have been down there in the first place."

"Tell Maestra Solis," Adriana said. "She's the most understanding."

Beto wondered whether Ms. Solis would yell at him again. He had just gotten back on her good side.

Adriana made them go to the maestra's office before their first period class. When they got there, there was a long line of students waiting. La Maestra was looking like she had too much to worry about even without the addition of a dead body in the basement.

"What do we do now?" Juan asked. "Should we tell the director?"

"No way!" Gonzalo said. "He's probably the one who put the body there in the first place. He and Mr. Silva."

"Don't be ridiculous," Adriana said. "But I agree about not talking to Director Contreras. I think we need to talk to someone friendlier than the director."

Beto noticed it was almost time for their class. And they had to be in class to get their homework, just in case there was a future for the school beyond this storm. They hurried to Mr. Stewart's classroom, only to meet most of the other students leaving the classroom.

"Crazy old Mr. Stewart is outside," Marisa explained. "He wants us to come out there."

Beto followed the rest of the class to where Mr. Stewart was marking the school building with wax pencils. He smiled when he saw the students coming towards him.

"This is going to be a big storm," he said. "And sea level is more than a foot higher than the last time we had a big hurricane. We are going to see some major effects."

He began handing out the wax pencils to the students.

"I want you to mark the level of the sand around the entire building. I'm expecting some major upheaval."

The students began marking ground level.

"Put a lot of wax on there," Mr. Stewart said, "There's going to be hours and hours of heavy rain."

The students rubbed harder and harder.

"Why don't we just take photos?" Marisa asked.

Mr. Stewart's eyebrows raised and he smiled. "Good idea, Miss Ramirez. You're in charge of photographing ground level from every direction. Then send those photos somewhere safe on the wăng luò. I'm not sure anything here is going to survive."

"Did he say he didn't think anything was going to survive?" Gonzalo asked.

Juan nodded, wide-eyed.

Mr. Stewart gathered up students who were not marking or photographing the buildings.

"We're going to survey the plants around the school

to see which ones survive," Mr. Stewart said. "Some of these plants have root systems that will hold this sand in place like nothing else you could imagine. This building may get torn off its foundations before some of these palm trees move. And those little black mangroves—nothing's going to move them."

The students worked non-stop until the bell rang. Beto was thinking there was still lots of work to do when he saw Sister Elizondo walk out of the classroom building towards the students counting and photographing small shrubs.

"I think those of you in my religious studies class can stay out here and keep working if you want," she said. "We're about to see what the power of God's creation can do. I can't think of anything more instructive to your spiritual development than this."

The sister began to help with the plant survey. Soon, several classes were out doing the same thing. Beto looked around at the busy landscape. It was amazing seeing everyone work together, especially since it was possible they would never all be together again.

The morning was hot and still. Whatever high winds were building up in the gulf, they were not yet affecting the coast.

As Beto worked with a group along the beach, he noticed a border patrol electrovan drive into the school's parking lot. Officer Clemente, the mean one, walked into the school building. Two other officers got out of the vehicle and stood in the parking lot watching the students.

It wasn't long before another electrovan pulled into

the parking lot followed by a Cruz Mining Company truck.

"What are they up to?" Beto asked Gonzalo and Juan.

Juan shrugged. "I've seen three drones already this morning. I think there's something big happening."

"Do you think we're in danger?" Beto asked.

"You don't think they could have found out about the body?" Gonzalo asked.

"The border patrol wouldn't be here for a dead body," Juan said. "They'd send the sheriff for that."

"Then what's going on?" Gonzalo asked.

"Let's go find out," Beto said.

They started to walk towards the parking lot, when The Voice began broadcasting.

"Okay, guys. You're *not* going to believe this, but the border patrol is here because *Cruz* told them Director Contreras is planning to use this storm as an excuse to *illegally* take foreign students out into the desert to establish a *permanent colony.*"

The director came out of the building with Officer Clemente. He looked angry. As the boys got closer, they could hear him yelling.

"How dare you accuse me and my students of illegal activity!" he said. "We have always conducted our school with the utmost care in regard to immigration law. Where is Lt. Noriega? He knows how careful we are."

Officer Clemente looked strangely happy that the director was losing his temper. She looked like she was about to arrest him, but Beto could not see what she was saying. Several officers began moving closer to Officer Clemente and the director. One had his hand on his handcuffs. Other officers noticed Beto and the students moving towards the parking lot and they moved to stop the students from getting any closer.

Fortunately, Maestra Solis walked out of the building just as the whole situation looked like it was about to explode.

"This is outrageous!" the director was saying.

"Please calm down," Clemente said. Beto noticed that one officer had a tiny red light glowing on his neurochip, indicating that he was making a video record of the director. The director was so angry in the moment, the video was going to look very incriminating.

Maestra Solis walked between the camera and the director.

"There is a very simple way to address your accusations, officer," the maestra said to Clemente. "The parents of most of our students are arriving in the next few hours to take them home. The rest of the students are traveling by bus with the staff to the mainland. Since every one of our foreign students has a visa, why don't you just stay here and examine everyone's paperwork as they go? We'll be happy to let you talk to each student and family as they leave."

Director Contreras smiled. "A very logical solution. Much preferable to the confusion Officer Clemente has been causing with her draconian tactics," he said.

Needless to say, Officer Clemente was annoyed by this suggestion. Maestra Solis smiled at the officer making the video.

Director Contreras took a deep breath and regained his composure.

"This is an excellent idea, maestra," he said. Then he looked at Officer Clemente. "Tell us how you would like us to proceed. We'll do whatever it takes to satisfy your suspicions so that we can get all these children to safety."

Clemente stationed officers in the parking lot, ready to take action if anything looked suspicious. She and several others went into the school building to set up an area near the school's office where they could check everyone's paperwork. As the situation calmed, the man in the Cruz Mining truck drove away, talking to someone on his neuro phone.

Beto was amazed at the way Maestra Solis took charge.

"Did you see how the maestra put Clemente in her place?" the Voice said. "She is impressive!"

Everyone agreed that the maestra seemed to have won the argument in the parking lot. However, now that every hall had a border patrol officer in it, Beto wasn't so sure. He looked through the front windows and saw more border patrol vehicles in the parking lot.

Gonzalo walked up to Beto. "This probably isn't a good time to mention the body in the basement," he said quietly.

"No. It would be a very bad time," Beto agreed.

Chapter 19 - Officer Clemente

In which Officer Clemente occupies the Lindheimer Academy and Beto sees the woman in white again.

Maestra Solis was angry about the armed officials everywhere in the school. She placed her teachers and staff in every hallway with instructions to make sure the officers did not harass the students. It seemed as if everyone had cameras focused on everyone else. Officer Clemente did her best to shut down every camera she did not control, but there were too many subtle ways the students could observe and record.

When Adriana came to the office with her paperwork, Officer Clemente even scanned Adriana's artificial eye. She held a scanner up to Adriana's face.

"Can you record data with that thing?" Clemente asked.

"This *thing*?" Adriana asked. "Do you mean my eye? No, there is no recording device. It is just so that I can see."

Clemente did not believe her. She carefully examined

Adriana's paperwork. Beto thought it was strange that the foreign students were required to carry physical documents in addition to having all their documents in electronic form in the government's database.

After Clemente looked at Adriana's papers, she scanned her biometric data. Then she asked Adriana a series of very specific questions. It was obvious she was trying to find something, anything, wrong. Adriana passed Officer Clemente's scrutiny.

When she was finished, Beto sat next to her on a sofa out of the way of all the examinations.

"This is crazy," Beto said. "They shouldn't be treating you so rudely."

"We're used to it," Adriana said. "Besides, what can we do? They have the power to do whatever they want to us. They can let us come here and get an education or say no and send us home. That's the way it is."

"What about 'liberty and justice for all?' What about 'all men are created equal?' Why do we have to learn all this stuff when the adults in charge obviously don't believe it?"

Adriana smiled. "Those are ideals, Beto. Of course, the typical adult can't live up to them all the time. But we have to keep striving for them. Maybe our generation will do better. They teach us this stuff because they want us to do better than they have."

By dinnertime, the school was almost empty. Adriana, Gonzalo, and Juan had gone home with their families. It was strange seeing them with brothers and sisters. For a while, it had seemed like the students at school were all the family any of them really had.

The nearly empty dining hall echoed with each movement as the few remaining students ate their meals in silence. Beto took his food out onto the plaza so he could sit alone and think about Adriana. He might never see her again.

The sky was completely clouded over and the constant breeze had returned. Every now and then, a stronger gust of wind would blow.

Marisa came out onto the plaza.

"What are you doing out here?" she asked.

"Watching the storm come in," Beto said. "If it's going to ruin my life, I might as well take time to see it and feel it."

"It's not going to ruin our lives," Marisa said. "I was being overly dramatic earlier. This building has survived hurricanes before."

"Not like this one, according to Mr. Stewart."

"We'll all be back," Marisa said. "One way or another, we'll survive. I mean, think about it. We're learning the skills humanity is going to need to survive in the long term. How sad would it be if one storm wrecked the director's entire project?"

"How long do you think the school will be closed after the storm?" Beto asked.

"A few weeks maybe," Marisa said. "If we're lucky."

Beto looked out into the dark gray sky over the ocean.

"Are you going to miss Adriana?" Marisa asked.

"Of course," Beto said."I'll miss this whole place. A few months ago I hated having to come here. But now, I have friends I'm going to miss. The teachers are actually interesting here. Odd, but interesting. And the field lab. What a great thing!"

"I know. To have an outdoor high school—it's the best idea ever," Marisa said.

"Do you think there's any truth to the rumor that the director is planning to start a colony out there?" Beto asked.

"I have no doubt he is," Marisa said. "Everything we do out there is intended to get us ready for staying out there and not coming back. But who he is planning to have stay out there is a mystery to me. Every homerista I have known has gone on to college—except Antonio and Rosario. But I imagine they'll go to college or get real jobs someday also."

"Will the director ever live out there, maybe?" Beto asked.

Marisa shook her head. "It's strange to say, but he's not that comfortable out there. No, whatever he is planning, it's for someone else."

Beto finished his food and started packing up his notebook and pen.

"What do you want to do in college?" Beto asked.

"Me?" Marisa said. "I'm not ready for college. I might want to help with the homeristas like Rosario. Or I might travel the world. I'm a doer, not a scholar. What about you?" Marisa asked.

"I'm just a sophomore. There's too much in front of me to even think about that."

They gazed at the coming storm for a while and then

went in to the dining hall to see what the other students were doing. The rest of the evening was spent playing games and talking. The quiet, intellectual students played chess. The other students joined in more boisterous activities, like karaoke and charades. Finally, when it was time for lights out, Beto went back to his room.

He couldn't sleep. The wind gusted through his windows. His mind was racing, thinking about all the ways this storm could change his life. Finally, he decided to go back down to the plaza and watch the storm.

It was against the rules to be out after hours, but who cared at this point? He put on dark clothes and then two layers of socks to keep his foot from making noise. He sat on the side of the fountain and looked up at the stars.

Out of the corner of his eye, he saw the light again. This time it floated down the second floor hallway. In an instant, Beto was on his feet and at the classroom doors. They were all locked. He ran to the auditorium door that Juan had rigged to stay unlocked, ran through the auditorium, through the dark foyer, and then quietly entered the great hallway.

There was no light floating down the hall. But Beto went down the hall in the direction he had seen the light go. He stopped at Ms. Lin's classroom. The sweet smell was there again. He looked in the classroom and saw nothing.

There has to be an explanation for the light! But what is it?

He went back out to the hallway. A loose sheet of paper fluttered on the floor as a gust of wind hit the building. Beto walked over and examined the paper. Someone had drawn a cartoon of a giant wave crashing over a small, rectangular building that looked like a child-sized version of the school. *Is this someone's idea of a joke?*

Having no idea where to go next, Beto walked upstairs to get a better view of the restless ocean. He was happy to notice he was walking very quietly—no tapping of his artificial foot.

At the very top of the stairs, the view of the ocean was breathtaking, even in the darkness. Beto could feel the impending power of the storm. Somehow the wind and the waves felt and sounded different. Beto could smell the salty scent of the gulf. And then something sweet. He looked up and down the hallway. He heard the sound of a chair being moved across the floor. Someone was here!

Slowly he moved to the far side of the hallway and began walking down the long length of the senior hallway. He carefully stayed in the shadows. The sweet smell lingered. Halfway down the hallway, he noticed that the director's office door was open. From across the hallway he looked in. At first he saw nothing unusual. Then he saw her! The woman in white was standing at the director's giant window looking out to sea.

Who was she? Beto was too far away to tell. Silently, he crossed the hallway to get closer. When he could touch the door of the director's office, he looked around the door. From the back, her hair was not as long as Beto had remembered. It fell just below her shoulders. She wore a simple, sleeveless night dress. Then she turned. It was Maestra Solis!

Silently she walked past the director's desk and to

the picture of the director's wife, Julia. The maestra stood perfectly still, gazing at the portrait. Then she lifted a hand and gently touched Julia's face. *What's going on?*

Beto heard a soft sound coming from the middle stairway. Someone was coming up the stairs. Beto moved behind the office door, deep in the shadows. Up the stairs walked Dr. Esquivel. She walked to the office door and looked in. She was inches from Beto. His heart raced. What would happen if they caught him spying on teachers in the middle of the night?

Fortunately, Dr. Esquivel's attention was focused elsewhere. She walked in the office, straight towards Maestra Solis. She put an arm around la maestra and moved her to a couch where both women sat, still looking at the portrait. Maestra Solis leaned her head on Dr. Esquivel's shoulders. The women spoke in quiet tones, and Beto could not understand what they were saying.

Not knowing what else to do, Beto decided to leave before he was discovered. He walked back down the stairs, all the way down to the plaza.

Chapter 20 - The Late Exit

In which Officer Clemente delays the evacuation of the school, which turns out to be a potentially deadly mistake.

By morning, the rain had started. The students had a quick breakfast and waited for the director to appear to give them their final instructions for their evacuation. The teachers paced impatiently as the director failed to appear on time.

Beto looked around the dining hall. Marisa was sitting with a couple of Korean girls. The Rwandan students were all at one table, talking in hushed tones. The two students from southern Mexico were sitting with them. Beto sat alone at the table where Adriana, Gonzalo, and Juan would have sat with him.

Finally, the director appeared.

"Our bus is ready to leave. However, we are still waiting for Officer Clemente to arrive to give us our final approval to evacuate. Students, please gather your belongings and meet back here in fifteen minutes. We will be ready to leave as soon as we are given permission."

The students quickly returned to the dorms. Beto

noticed a large electrobus and the school's electrovan waiting in the otherwise empty parking lot. The rain was falling harder now. Beto grabbed his two bags and headed back to the dining hall. The wind was now driving the rain hard against the building. As the boys left their dorm, Mr. Silva was there to make sure the windows and doors were all securely closed. The first floor windows had all been covered with polymerboard.

By 9:30 a.m., all the students and staff were ready to go. Antonio and Mr. Stewart had loaded sack lunches into the bus, along with water for the trip. Rain beat against the windows. And still, there was no sign of Officer Clemente.

Finally, just after 10:00, two U.S. Border Patrol vehicles pulled into the parking lot. Officer Clemente and two other officers set up their visa inspection procedure in the dining hall. They checked paperwork. They checked all the luggage of all the students and staff. They searched the bus and the electrovan the school had rented. It was 11:35 a.m. by the time it was all over. Director Contreras had been going crazy with the delay, as the hurricane drew closer and closer. Outside, the wind had already reached 60 kilometers per hour.

But Officer Clemente was not yet ready to release the students. She wanted to search the building one last time. She and another officer walked through every room of every building with Mr. Silva.

"What is she looking for?" Marisa asked Beto. "She's endangering all of us, and for what?"

Beto shrugged.

Finally, Officer Clemente allowed the students

to board the bus. In all, there were fourteen students plus Antonio, Rosario, and Grace. Ms. Lin and Sister Elizondo also rode with the students. Director Contreras, Maestra Solis, and Dr. Esquivel drove together in the electrovan. Mr. Silva and Mr. Stewart were staying behind to tend to the building.

Antonio was driving, though how he could see through the heavy rain was a mystery to Beto. The flat landscape had so much water standing on it that it was difficult to tell where the road ended and where the soft, sandy shoulder of the road began.

The border patrol vehicles sped off into the gray distance, leaving the two school vehicles to slowly proceed down the old park road. When the bus came to a low water crossing, Antonio slowed to a near-stop. The water came halfway up the tires as the bus splashed through and came up the other side.

"We won't be able to make it if the water gets much deeper," Antonio yelled back to Sister Elizondo, who was sitting just a row back. The wind and rain were so loud that normal conversation was impossible.

"How far until we reach the highway?" Sister Elizondo asked.

"Twenty miles," Antonio answered.

The bus continued through the storm. There were a few other low-water crossings, but none were as bad as the first had been. Ms. Lin and Sister Elizondo handed out the lunches and the students ate quietly. They all seemed pretty overwhelmed by the storm.

Half an hour later, the bus came to a stop. Marisa

moved to Beto's seat and sat beside him.

"What's going on?" she asked. Beto shrugged.

"There's a water crossing in front of us, but I can't tell how deep it is," Antonio said.

The teachers looked out the windshield, but could see no depth marker.

"I'll go out and check," Rosario said.

"Are you sure?" Sister Elizondo said. "It's horrible out there."

"It's either that or turn back," Rosario said.

Antonio opened the door. Rosario walked out into the rain and slowly made her way to where the water was running over the road.

"I can't tell how deep it is," she yelled back to the bus.

She looked around the brush on the side of the road and found a long branch. She used the branch to feel the bottom of the road through the murky water. Slowly, she made her way across. At the deepest the water was only about two feet deep. Antonio thought he could make it through.

Director Contreras walked up to the bus under an umbrella. He was getting pretty soaked even with that little bit of protection. He, Antonio, and Rosario discussed the situation and they decided to go forward.

"If we get stuck, everyone will get out off the bus," Antonio instructed the students. "It will be better to get wet than to be stuck in a bus being swept away by flood water. Look around you and find the emergency window exits near the back of the bus. If we have to exit, we'll all go back to the electrovan, and they can shuttle us back to the school."

Beto wasn't sure this sounded like a good plan, but Antonio proceeded forward. Marisa grabbed Beto's hand and held it tightly. The bus made it through with no problem. The electrovan followed.

"Sorry," Marisa said, releasing Beto's hand. "I got nervous there for a second."

"Me too," Beto answered.

That was the worst of the crossings for quite some time. It seemed like the road was crossing higher ground. But a few miles later, they saw flashing lights in front of them. As the bus approached the lights they saw that it was a border patrol vehicle. It seemed to have gone off the road and gotten stuck in the mud.

Antonio stopped the bus. Officer Clemente, drenched by the rain, walked up to the bus. Antonio opened the door.

"My vehicle's stuck," she said. "I have a chain. I think you can probably pull it out."

"Are you sure you want to do that?" Antonio asked. "The storm is getting worse. We could just give you a ride."

"Let's just try it," Officer Clemente said. "It'll take five minutes at the most."

Rosario jumped out and helped with the chain. The bus pulled forward and sat in the middle of the highway as the chain was attached. Antonio revved the electric engine. Officer Clemente hit her accelerator and her wheels spun, but her vehicle did not move. Antonio revved the engine again. The result was the same. He backed up the bus a little. Then he accelerated forward. The bus moved forward and then came to a quick stop as the chain drew tight.

Officer Clemente came to the bus door again.

"I don't think that vehicle is going anywhere until we can get help," Antonio said.

Clemente reluctantly agreed.

"Where's your other vehicle?" Antonio asked.

"They headed south on the park road," Clemente said. "I radioed them and told them to not try to make it back here. I'll call into the station and let them know I'm abandoning the vehicle."

"Serves her right," Marisa said, adding some insult at the end, which was lost in the noise of the wind and rain.

Clemente walked back to her vehicle in the rain. Beto was kind of happy to see her looking so miserable. However, he wasn't so happy to think she was going to be traveling with them.

By the time Clemente made it back to the bus, she was completely soaked, her legs covered in mud. While standing in the bus's entry she removed her boots and emptied the water out of them. She tried to squeegee her shirt and trousers a little, then made her way to the back of the bus. She left a trail of water down the center of the bus.

Beto knew every student had their bags packed with dry clothes, but no one offered her anything. Antonio moved the bus forward down the road. Miles later he came to a stop again. This time there was a low-water crossing clearly too deep to cross.

Both vehicles parked in the center of the road and Director Contreras came into the bus so that all the adults could confer. There were no other routes off the island, unless they traveled all the way back to the school and headed south.

"How far have we come?" Sister Elizondo asked.

"About fifteen miles," Antonio said.

"Could we hike to the highway?" Rosario asked. "It's only five miles."

"We could, but there's no guarantee anyone will find us," Antonio said. "And who is going to have room to transport this many people?"

"I think we should turn back and take shelter in the school," the director said. "It will be safer there than in either of these vehicles."

Everyone agreed. And everyone remembered the precious hours they had wasted waiting for the Border Patrol to give them permission to leave. But no one said this aloud.

"So, we're stuck on the island?" Marisa whispered to Beto.

"I think so," Beto said.

"Do you think that old building will stand?"

"It's not going anywhere," Beto said.

It took quite some time for Antonio to turn the bus around. Rosario had to get out in the rain again to guide him so that he didn't get stuck in the mud. By the time they were headed south, it was getting very dark. Sunset was hours away, but it seemed like nighttime was already falling upon them. Beto felt panic and fear in his gut.

"It looks like the ocean is right there by the road," Marisa said.

The waves were rolling up onto the shoulder.

"That looks really bad," Beto said.

Marisa walked up the aisle and showed Ms. Lin how close the water was. Ms. Lin stood and pointed it out to Antonio.

"Believe me, I've been watching that myself," Antonio said.

The bus seemed to be going slower and slower. And then it stopped. It was another low-water crossing that was too deep to cross.

Officer Clemente moved to the front of the bus.

"What now?" she said.

"Now we're stuck on a narrow island in a giant storm," Antonio said. "Let's check the maps to find the highest ground near here. Fortunately, we still have our wăng luò connection."

Antonio turned on the bus's monitor and synced his neuro chip to it. Then he displayed a local topo map.

"We're here," he said, pointing to a point on the road. "The school is still more than ten miles away. The road is a little higher in a couple of miles if we can make this crossing on foot."

"You're suggesting we hike to higher ground?" Officer Clemente said.

"If we stay here, the bus could get swamped then swept away," Antonio said. "Once it gets dark, we won't be able to tell what is happening."

Clemente pointed to the map. "The road is a few feet higher if we turn back about a half mile. A few feet in a storm like this could make a lot of difference."

"The question is, do we hike on foot to higher ground or stay with the bus and get it as high as we can," Director Contreras said.

"Let's check the temperature," Antonio said. "These

kids could get hypothermia if they're out in the rain all night."

The temperature was going to drop into the 60's overnight, according to the wǎng luò.

"We need to stay dry," Antonio said. "That temperature doesn't sound cold, but once someone is wet, they lose heat fast. We won't make it out there. We need to stay in the bus."

"And if the water starts to move the bus?" Sister Elizondo said.

"Then we hike to higher ground and pray," Antonio said.

They turned the bus around once again and drove to the highest point on the road. The waves were not so near.

Antonio shut down the bus's motor.

"Okay," he said. "This is where we'll be for the next twelve to twenty-four hours. The storm is going to pass over us. We're fifteen feet above normal sea level. The storm surge could be almost that high."

"So you're saying we could be underwater when the hurricane hits full force?" Marisa said. She looked nervous.

Antonio nodded. "If the surge is higher than fifteen feet, there will be no land around here. But that is unlikely to happen."

This announcement produced gasps of terror. Director Contreras stood up.

"Everybody stay calm. We are in a difficult situation, but we are fortunate to have the leadership of Antonio and Rosario and Grace. If anyone can survive out here, they can. Until this storm passes, we will do what they say. Just listen carefully and work as a group. In a few hours, we'll be safely through this."

"If it wasn't for her," Marisa said, pointing to Officer Clemente, "we'd be safely out of here."

There were several noises of agreement.

"No, it is not anyone's fault but my own," the director said. "It was my job to get all of you safely out of the storm's path long before there was any danger. Passing blame will not help us right now. I am the director of the school, and I am the only one you may blame. Officer Clemente was simply doing her job. Now, not another word of blame. We need to think about how we are going to face this storm."

Antonio had the group list all of their assets. They had almost no food. They had warm, dry clothes, but much of it was stowed in the storage bins of the bus that could only be accessed from the outside. Officer Clemente and Rosario, who were both wet already, volunteered to go out and bring in the dry gear. There would also be a little food students had stashed in their luggage.

"What if we have to use the restroom?" Marisa asked.

"You'll have to get wet," Rosario said. "Wear as little clothing as you can when you go outside and get into dry clothes as soon as you get back in. We'll try to make some private area up in the front of the bus for changing clothes when we go in and out."

"This is crazy," Marisa said.

Beto agreed.

"I do not want to die out here," Marisa said.

Maestra Solis overheard this remark. She stood up.

"Listen everyone. We are in danger. We all know that," she said. "But we have very good leadership, as Director Contreras has pointed out. Now, it is our job to not make ourselves miserable. We can be scared and angry—which will make the next few hours truly difficult. Or we can choose to think of this as an adventure, a great challenge we have to face together."

She smiled a very reassuring smile.

"From now on, I want no negative comments, not even under your breath. In fact, I don't want you to even think negative comments. There is not much positive in this situation, but let's find it and enjoy it. We have friends on this bus. We have some interesting people. Antonio and Rosario can tell us stories about the most challenging situations they've faced before. I'm sure Dr. Esquivel has stories to tell, as a mythologist. And Officer Clemente probably has some interesting and exciting adventures. Let's focus on the good and interesting things we have here with us."

The students visibly relaxed as the maestra spoke.

"What do you want to hear first?" she said. "Should we start with Antonio and Rosario's adventures?"

The students were actually a little enthusiastic about this.

"Rosario!" Marisa yelled. "Tell us something amazing!"

There was clapping as Rosario stood up.

"Actually, I've been through a hurricane before. I was working in a mountain village in the Dominican Republic, helping to build a water system, when the hurricane hit. We were living in very simple huts and they didn't give much protection from the rain. Believe me, this bus is a lot nicer to sit through a hurricane in."

"But you said you were in a mountain village," said Kim, one of the Korean students. "High above sea level."

"True," Rosario said. "But up there, the danger is mudslides. Your hut may slide down the mountain. Or a mountain of mud may slide down on top of you. I think we're better off here."

"How long can you swim?" said Hope, another one of the Korean students.

Rosario grabbed one of the seat cushions and yanked it off the seat.

"With one of these, I plan to swim for a long, long time," she said.

The students laughed. But Beto made a mental note—use the seat cushions for flotation.

Rosario kept the group entertained for a long time. Maestra Solis kept asking questions about every detail. She was obviously trying to extend the conversation, but it was working. Everyone felt a little more relaxed. When an especially strong gust of wind hit the bus, they all tensed up again, but they were soon laughing.

By the time Rosario had described just about every person in the little village in the Dominican Republic it was very dark outside. Antonio kept the bus lights off to conserve power.

Chapter 21 - Unwelcome Visitors

In which a new threat appears, and Beto is unexpectedly helpful.

When Rosario was finished, Maestra Solis called on Antonio to tell the story of one of his adventures. Beto noticed that Antonio had been in a very intense conversation with the director when he was called upon. It took him a few seconds to realize what was being asked.

"Just a second," he said. "First, I'd like to talk to Officer Clemente."

Office Clemente went to the front of the bus and after a short conversation, Antonio opened the exit door and she went out into the rain.

"What's going on?" Marisa asked.

"We saw some loose dogs or something running outside the bus. Animals are just as disoriented as we are. Officer Clemente went out to encourage them to leave the area."

Everyone on the bus tried to see what was happening outside but the rain and the darkness made it difficult to see anything. Beto thought he saw the light of a flashlight behind the bus but other than that brief swipe of light there was nothing else. And then, they heard the discharge of a gun. The sound caused panic on the bus and as Maestra Solis tried to calm everyone down, there was a loud thump on the exit door. Antonio ran to the door and opened it.

"It's Officer Clemente," he said, disappearing down the exit steps.

When he reappeared, he was helping her up the steps.

"She's been injured! I need the first aid kit."

Grace Nkazi grabbed the kit and hurried to the front of the bus.

"What happened?" she asked.

Everyone near the front of the bus could see there was blood on Officer Clemente. Grace rolled up the officer's sleeves and began to clean her injured arms.

"Coyotes," Officer Clemente said. "A whole pack of them."

"These are deep wounds," Grace said.

"I tried to run them off, but they wouldn't stay away. And then they surrounded me and attacked. It was terrifying. I managed to grab my gun but one of them bit my arm. I got one desperate shot off and then dropped the gun. The sound scared them away but I couldn't find my gun in the water and I didn't want to stay on my hands and knees looking for it. I ran back to the bus."

"These injuries are bad," Grace said. "And your legs are bleeding, too."

"There were so many of them. And they were so

fast," Officer Clemente said.

"Let's clean these wounds and stop the bleeding," Grace said. "You just sit on the front seat here and I'll take care of it."

"What do we do now?" Marisa asked.

"We stay in the bus," Director Contreras said.

"And if someone needs to use the restroom?" Marisa said. "Antonio said we could be here for a day or more."

"She's right," Sister Elizondo said. "With this many people on the bus, someone is going to have to relieve themselves sooner or later."

"Okay, let's think about this," Antonio said. "Coyotes rarely attack people. They must be panicking. They'll probably move on. And even if they remain nearby, I'll bet they'll be less likely to attack if several people go outside together."

"So, we should go to the bathroom in groups?" Marisa asked.

"A gun would be useful right now, but the one we had is lost in the darkness," Rosario said. "And we didn't bring our bows."

"Rosario and I will escort anyone who needs to go outside," Antonio said. "We'll protect ourselves with whatever we can find."

He looked around.

"The fire extinguisher," he said. "That could be helpful."

He sounded doubtful.

Beto raised his hand.

"I have my sling," he said, sheepishly. "And a bunch

of projectiles Juan made."

Antonio paused.

"Okay, then. We'll add you to guard duty," Rosario said. "Does anyone have anything else that could be used as a weapon?"

No one replied.

"Beto, get up here and let's talk about how that sling works," Rosario said.

Sister Elizondo joined Grace in helping tend to Officer Clemente's wounds. From what Beto could see, the wounds looked bad—very long and very deep.

"Excuse me, ma'am, but it looks like you're going into shock," Grace said to Officer Clemente. "We need to get her some dry clothes and some water to drink."

Marisa appeared and handed over her flannel shirt and a canteen. Antonio pulled Rosario and Grace to the driver's section of the bus.

"Here's the plan," he said. "No one goes outside unless absolutely necessary. When someone does need to go outside, two of us go with them. Beto, is that sling going to be any help? Honestly?"

"We've gotten much better with them compared to when we first started," Beto said. "I think it's better than nothing."

"I hope we don't have to find out," Antonio said.

Once Grace had finished with first aid, they walked Officer Clemente to the back of the bus and tried to make her as comfortable as possible.

"Shall we continue with the stories?" Maestra Solis

asked.

"Excellent idea," Director Contreras said. "That might help us regain our sense of calm. Antonio, do you have a story for us?"

"Okay," Antonio said, standing up. "Let me tell you of the time I almost drowned, kayaking in a river that was swollen with floodwater. It was bad idea. I was swept off my kayak and then sucked into a limestone hole that the water was falling through. My legs made it through the hole but my hips got stuck. I was completely submerged and all the current of the river was holding me down."

"What did you do?" Marisa asked.

"Somehow I forced myself through. I had giant bruises on my hips and thighs. But once I was through, the current dumped me into a big, calm pool of water. I swam to the surface, because I had lost my PFD, and I survived to kayak another day."

"That sounds terrifying," Marisa said.

"It happened so fast, I didn't have time to be scared," Antonio said. "But I should not have been on the river that day, facing unknown conditions. The lesson I learned was that I am not invincible. There are things in nature much more powerful than I am. I survived by luck that day. Since then I've worked hard to try to be smart enough to keep the odds on my side in tricky situations."

"Good story," Maestra Solis said.

"Well, Rosario's was better," Antonio said. "At least she was doing something worthwhile in the Dominican Republic. I was just being stupid."

"But you learned a lesson," the maestra said. She

BETO AND THE APOCALYPSE

looked at the students. They were all pretty peaceful, even though the bus was hit repeatedly by strong gusts of wind. Antonio went to the back of the bus and took Rosario's place by Officer Clemente. Even in the dark, Beto noticed the officer's skin looked very pale.

"Are you all ready for sleep or do you want another story?" the maestra said.

"More stories!" several students yelled.

The maestra looked around at the adults. They all seemed to agree.

"Dr. Esquivel?" the maestra said. "Do you have anything for us?"

Dr. Esquivel smiled bashfully.

"Tell us about the mythology of the school that you've been working on," Kim called out.

"Well, I'm not sure I'm ready to talk about the school. Director Contreras and I are still working on that."

The students groaned.

"But I will tell you one of the best myths I know."

"Wait," Antonio said. "I'm afraid Officer Clemente is getting too cold. We need to get her out of these wet clothes."

Grace and Rosario collected dry clothes from among the girls' luggage. They helped Officer Clemente change, and then sat on either side of her with their arms around her to warm her up.

Antonio carefully examined everyone in the bus for signs of hypothermia. "Watch your friends for warning signs like blue lips, cold skin, shivering that goes on for a long time and then stops. No one should stay wet. We have

238

enough dry clothes for everyone to stay dry as long as we are in the bus."

Antonio assigned everyone buddies and made them check each other using the few flashlights they had. At the moment, everyone except Officer Clemente was doing well.

"Okay, Dr. Esquivel," Antonio said. "We're ready for your story."

As Dr. Esquivel prepared to tell her tale, Beto noticed Antonio giving Officer Clemente something to drink from a flask.

Chapter 22 - Stories in the Dark

In which Dr. Celeste Esquivel tells the story of the trickster.

"I've heard versions of this story from many different parts of the world. The themes seem to be almost universal. But I'll tell you the version that I was told by a Mayan storyteller, who descended from a long line of storytellers.

"It begins with a magical, heavenly family that at one time lived among humans. This family consisted of seven brothers and their little sister. They appeared one day in a little village and the humans could tell they were different, even though they looked like ordinary people. They were very friendly and kind and completely trusting. And they soon demonstrated their good intentions by helping the village with their extraordinary knowledge.

"In some cultures, it was this family who brought fire to humans. More often it is said they brought a deep understanding of the medicinal use of plants.

"When they were asked who they were and where they came from, they would just point to the sky and say they were visitors who had decided to learn more about humans.

"For many years they lived with the villagers and observed everything they did. They were curious about everything—food, tools, old stories. It seemed that they were as interested in learning from the humans as the humans were interested in learning from them.

"Are we talking about aliens?" Marisa asked.

Dr. Esquivel laughed.

"Possibly," she said. "Aliens or gods or angels or demons. But they were visitors from another place, so, literally speaking, aliens may be the best term.

"Regardless of what you call them, they lived peacefully and happily among the humans for some time. And the humans benefited greatly from their presence. Although the visitors would not even touch weapons, the typical enemies of the people of this village ceased to attack them. Before the visitors came, raiding among villages was common. But now there was peace, and with this peace abundant crops and fruits gathered from the surrounding forest.

"Uh oh. This won't last," Marissa said.

"I told you it was a universal story," Dr. Esquivel said. "You can all probably guess how this is going to end."

Everyone nodded. Everyone except Officer Clemente, who was getting some color back in her face but still looked very sleepy.

"One day, another visitor appeared in the village. He was known to the villagers because he was a trickster that came and went. He was never serious trouble to anyone, but he was known to steal small amounts of food, cause arguments, and break things due to his inordinate curiosity. He was a good storyteller and sometimes helpful, but he was always trouble.

"And he was very interested in the other visitors. He followed them everywhere. And they didn't seem to mind his presence. The villagers thought this was strange because the visitors seemed very wise. Surely they would know the trickster was going to cause trouble. But they showed no sign of distrust or caution.

"One day, the visitors were with a family and they noticed the children had constructed a swing made of rope tied to a tree branch. The visitors were fascinated by the sight of the children swinging through the air. They watched the children play for hours. But the trickster began to appear bored.

"'I've seen swings before and this is not a particularly good one,' he said. 'In fact, I can show you how to build a really impressive swing.'

"Everyone was interested in this and so they followed the trickster into the forest. He found a place where the trees were very tall and not very close together. He went to a pair of trees that grew near to each other and asked the villagers to bring him the longest ropes they had.

"When the ropes were brought to him, he instructed one boy to climb as high as he could into one of the trees and then tie the rope securely around the trunk. He gave a girl another rope and told her to climb the other tree and do the same. When the ropes were in place, he took the ends and tied them together so that they hung near the ground.

He took another rope and fashioned a little net that served as a seat once it was attached to the long ropes and he invited one of the village children to sit on it.

"The resulting swing was amazing. The village children loved it. They took turns playing with it and sometimes there were long lines of children waiting to swing. There was no possibility of making a second swing because these were the longest ropes in the village and they were tied to the tallest trees. But no one seemed to mind waiting for their turn because the swing was so much fun.

"The visitors were also impressed by the swing. In fact, the little female visitor enjoyed the swing as much as any of the human children. Her brothers always stayed near her when she swung because they were afraid of what might happen if she swung too high and fell.

"As time went on, the swing remained a favorite pastime for the children, but life in the village went on. However, every evening the little girl visitor made a point of swinging for at least a little while. It was her favorite thing.

"Hunting season came and, although the visitors never ate animal flesh, they were interested in how the villagers hunted. One day the villagers were planning a long hunting trip that would take several days. The visitors wanted to go along, but it was considered too dangerous a trip for the very old and the very young, and so the little girl visitor had to stay behind. The trickster also decided to stay behind. He said he had been on many hunts before and this one did not interest him.

"Oh no," Marisa said. "This is going to be trouble."

Dr. Esquivel nodded.

"Trouble indeed," she said. "The first evening, when the little girl wanted to swing, the trickster offered to go with her. The girl swung as usual and the trickster pushed her a little higher than normal.

"'Be careful,' the girl said. 'My brothers have warned me not to swing too high.'

"'Well, of course, we won't make you go too high,' the trickster said. 'But I'm sure you can go just a little higher. And besides, this is a very large and very strong swing. It would be a shame to not see how far you can go.'

"He pushed the girl higher and higher and no matter how much she protested, he always said, 'Just a little more.'

"Finally she was swinging high above most of the treetops and she was very scared. The trickster said, 'Just one more push,' and he sent her flying higher still. And just as she reached the top of the swing's arc, one of the ropes snapped and the girl went flying through the air."

"Oh my god!" Rosario gasped. She'd been listening very intently.

"The girl looked down and realized that if she fell she would very likely die. And so she grabbed for the sky and she hung suspended from there. Because heavenly beings can do that. And there she remained because she knew no way to get back to earth and she wasn't sure she wanted to go back even if she could.

"The trickster now knew he was in trouble. He fled from the village as fast as he could go. And when the brothers returned, they met a bunch of concerned villagers.

"'We don't know what happened,' they said, 'but

the trickster is gone and so is your sister.'

"The brothers were both angry and worried. They searched everywhere in the village for their sister, but they could find no trace of her. They were about to give up and go to track down the trickster when night fell. And from the sky, they heard the voice of their little sister.

"She explained all that had happened. The brothers were angry at the trickster, but they were also angry at the villagers for allowing the trickster to remain in the village so long and to leave him alone with their sister. That night they decided to return to the heavens. And they never returned to the village.

"The villagers looked up into the night sky and they could see the seven brothers and their sister, but no matter how they called to them, their calls were never answered."

Dr. Esquivel leaned back in her seat. There was silence in the electrobus, except for the beating of the rain.

"Hmm," Marisa said. "They walked with the gods until the first sin came into the world. It sounds almost biblical."

Dr. Esquivel nodded. "People often look back to a golden age when things were better, magical, less threatening. And they wonder why they cannot manage to make it back to that place or those days," she said.

Beto thought for a few moments. "I wonder, since we're the first students in this new school, if future students will look back to us as their mythical ancestors. Maybe they'll tell great stories of our exploits."

Antonio laughed.

"You're gonna have to get a lot better with that sling

before anyone tells stories about you," he said.

Beto nodded. Sadly, that was true.

"That's an odd story for you to tell, Dr. Esquivel," the director said. "Because of all of us here, you are the most likely candidate to be the trickster. You are neither a student nor a teacher. You are the outsider that has been welcomed in."

"I was aspiring to be more like the heavenly family, but maybe the trickster is also a possibility," she said. "I hope my work doesn't bring an end to the golden age of your school."

She said this in a light-hearted way, but it made Beto's skin prickle. Was there something dangerous about this woman and her work?

"Director Contreras makes a good point, though. One way of looking at this story is for each person to see oneself as the trickster. Whenever we look deeply into anything, we tend to ruin its magic, even as we learn about it."

Marissa nodded. "It could be that we are creating a whole school of tricksters and setting them loose on society," she said.

Beto noticed the Director and Dr. Esquivel exchange a knowing look, even as they politely laughed at this comment.

Marisa leaned over to Beto and whispered, "Did you notice that Dr. Esquivel's story reveals nothing about herself?"

"What do you mean?" Beto said.

"Antonio and Rosario told us personal stories, things they had done," Marisa said. "We're here, possibly about to die together, and still Dr. Esquivel is aloof and secretive."

Chapter 23 - Secrets

In which Dr. Celeste Esquivel reveals several secrets.

It was now perfectly dark outside the bus. The director kept opening the bus door to check the ground outside, making sure the storm surge hadn't risen enough to float the bus, but it was now almost impossible to tell what was happening out there. Besides, if the bus started to float, where would they go anyway? There was no higher ground.

The students were hungry for more stories from Dr. Esquivel. They wanted something to think about other than the danger all around them.

"Now, tell us about ourselves," Marisa said. "Who knows what's going to happen tonight? At the very least, you can share a little about things we ought to know about our own story."

Dr. Esquivel looked back at Director Contreras. The director nodded.

"Perhaps it is time to begin to tell the story," he said.

"All of the story?" Dr. Esquivel asked.

"Whatever is necessary."

Dr. Esquivel looked up at the ceiling and drew in a deep breath. She looked towards Maestra Solis.

"Are you okay with this?" Dr. Esquivel asked.

La Maestra nodded.

"Where do I start?" Dr. Esquivel said. "First, let me get me comfortable."

She sat on a seat with her back to the side of the bus and looked out at the students, who were now listening intently.

"After my first round of interviews, I found the school to be a very interesting place for international students. The students came here to learn English, get a good education, and prepare for college. All of you were very serious about your studies and very serious about making this campus a big family."

Her eyes darted to Sister Elizondo.

"And the students were very serious about faith, and how that creates a positive environment. It gives them a good code for living together well—to help each other, to be thinking of the people around them and not just themselves. It creates a supportive and happy family—at least the way it's practiced here. I can't say that's always been my experience of the church.

"Those results weren't surprising. They were good, but not surprising. I thought the scientific and outdoor programs might be a little more unusual. But at first, they too seemed very ordinary. The field lab here functioned much like a sports program at other schools. It gave students a means to express their physical intelligence. It supplied another strong small-group that faced common challenges and had common goals.

"But as I pressed more deeply, I found some truly extraordinary things about the field lab program. Underneath the college prep veneer of the school, there was another, secret reason for the school's existence."

Dr. Esquivel glanced at Officer Clemente. Clemente was now comfortable and warm, but she was listening intently. Beto noticed that Antonio had continued to give her drinks from the flask.

"Before I talk about the secret reason for the school's existence, let me go back a lot further. Director Contreras has always had an interest in the natural world. He has always believed in getting people out into nature and having hands-on experiences. That's why he started the field lab program five years ago. But when his wife died, everything changed."

"There are things you need to know about Mrs. Contreras. She was an immigrant from Mexico. *Legal*," she emphasized, looking at Officer Clemente. "But most of her family could not get permission to come to the U.S. So, she was isolated from them much of the time. Several members of her family tried to come to the U.S. illegally. She lost a cousin who had been very close to her during a smuggling operation that went wrong. The girl died of heat stroke, locked in a truck that had been abandoned when the smugglers driving it decided it was more important to protect the drugs they were carrying than the people.

"And then, in her home village, a big chemical company discovered a large natural gas deposit. The whole village became a giant industrial operation. This brought in lots of jobs and money, but care was not taken to keep the operation safe. Julia's mother and many of the native families were exposed to huge amounts of very dangerous chemicals. It wasn't long before Julia's mother fell ill. In the middle of all of that mess, Julia went home to care for her mother. And, of course, she began breathing the same poisonous air and drinking the same poisonous water.

"Her mother died horribly and painfully. And then when Julia returned to the U.S., she soon discovered the same tumors were growing in her as those that had killed her mother. Julia decided to end her own life rather than face the pain and disfigurement she had seen her mother go through. One summer, she and the director took a little weekend vacation to the coast. She never returned. She drowned herself in the gulf."

The students were transfixed by this story. Beto felt tears welling up. Dr. Esquivel looked around the bus and made eye contact with the adults.

"Julia had an older sister who came to the U.S. for college and found a job as an ESL teacher, and eventually was given U.S. citizenship."

Dr. Esquivel looked at Maestra Solis.

"That sister, you all know as Naomi Solis, your maestra."

The students, and most of the adults, gasped.

"After Julia died, the central idea of this school was formed by Director Contreras and Maestra Solis. This is not a college prep school, at its heart. College will prepare you to become part of the industrial world that destroyed their family. This school is preparing you to oppose and subvert that world."

Chapter 24 - The Storm Ends

In which Officer Clemente reveals two secrets of her own.

The wind continued to rock the bus. The passengers were silent. Beto remembered watching Maestra Solis stare at Julia's portrait at midnight in the nearly-empty school building. It seems that both leaders in the school were still haunted by the memories of this dead woman.

Director Contreras was still thinking about Dr. Esquivel's statement—that the school was not, at its core, a college prep school.

"Explain what you mean by oppose and subvert," Director Contreras said.

"Yeah, and how do we students fit into the plan?" Marisa said. "And just what is the plan?"

Dr. Esquivel smiled.

"Oh, yes, there is a plan. First, the school focuses on the natural world—knowing it, understanding it, caring for it. The outside world is preoccupied with controlling and using the world to build up monetary wealth.

"Second, the school focuses on self-sufficiency. The outside world is trying to make everyone reliant on the neural net so we can't think for ourselves.

"In simpler terms, the outside world is interested in turning the world into a giant machine to serve a few wealthy people. The natural world and the working people of the world are simply resources to be exploited. Your school sees the world as full of living beings, including non-human beings, that deserve all the respect and attention that every human deserves. In order to accomplish this, you are learning to listen to and nurture the natural world instead of using it for your pleasure."

The director nodded.

"What the hell does that all mean?" Officer Clemente asked.

"It means I see Antonio and Rosario as more successful than the students I have sent on to college and law school and medical school. The homeristas know what it is to be human," the director said.

"There's a lot more to the story than that," Clemente said. "I've tracked your activities for almost two hundred miles through the desert. You're setting up safe havens out there for a lot of people. Maybe enough for your entire school."

The director laughed.

"If you think we have enough resources for two hundred students to survive in the desert, then you know nothing of the desert. I would like to see people living out there, but at most we've prepared for two dozen."

"And where are your two dozen people going

to come from?" Clemente said. "You want to know why we've been watching your school so closely? We're trying to protect your students."

"Do you honestly think I am proposing to kidnap students from my school?" the director said. "Do you think that because these students are from Mexico or Rwanda that their parents have forgotten about them? My students are exactly what they seem; they are students who are here for a good education."

"Does that include the ones from the Cavazos Aguilar cartel?" Clemente said.

Wait, Beto thought. Those are Adriana's names.

The director shook his head. "You obviously know something I do not."

"You have several students who are related to the Cavazos Aguilar organized crime family," Clemente said, raising her voice.

"I can't speak to that," the director said. "Students apply to our school and they are approved to come by the U.S. State Department. If they are related to criminals, no one has ever informed me."

"And even if they are related to someone in organized crime, these students are just children," Maestra Solis said. "Giving them an education isn't a crime."

Officer Clemente rolled her eyes. "Even if you don't know who these students are, it doesn't mean they can't use your school as a way to forward their own agenda," she said.

"If their agenda is educating children and teaching young people to understand nature and to be self-reliant, then we are guilty!" the director said. "I can assure you that nothing else is happening in my school."

"I hope you're right," Officer Clemente said. "But it's my job to make sure."

"Is it also your job to put pressure on us in the name of Cruz Mining Company?" Rosario asked. She was still sitting with one arm around Officer Clemente to keep her warm.

"Don't even talk to me about them," Officer Clemente said. "I've spent more time than I care to admit being manipulated by them. They're willing to do anything they can to close your school down. And they may have enough money and enough lawyers to do it."

"Why do they want to close us down?" Antonio asked.

"You're the biggest obstacle preventing them from owning this whole county and doing whatever they want," Officer Clemente said. "They're the only big employer in the area. And people always want jobs."

The bus shuddered from the hurricane winds.

"This storm may remove that obstacle once and for all," Rosario said.

Antonio went to the bus door to check conditions outside. He couldn't see much, so he opened the door. The wind and rain swept in violently as he took a step outside the bus.

"Antonio, what are you doing out there?" Rosario yelled into the wind.

Antonio came back in, soaked. "We're still above the water," he said. "But just barely. There's water all around us."

"What do we do?" Rosario said.

"We wait," Antonio said.

Dr. Esquivel stood. "This storm really emphasizes the amazing story of the school," she said. "Everything is stacked up against you. Industry wants you shut down. The government scrutinizes you, even to the point of putting students in danger."

Officer Clemente started to object.

"No offense, officer, but you are part of the reason we are stuck here. It was your fear of the counter-cultural aspects of the school that caused you to delay evacuation."

Dr. Esquivel looked at Director Contreras and Maestra Solis.

"But with all of these opposing forces, you still have the courage to teach what you believe in. And students come from all over the world to learn from you. And now, nature itself is right on the verge of crushing you, but you still have hope. Whatever happens tonight will not change the power of your vision."

The director looked out the window. The bus rocked. He thought he heard waves hitting the undercarriage of the bus.

Director Contreras was solemn. "I'm not so sure about that. I think this hurricane could totally erase us from the earth tonight. I think it is out of our hands."

More time passed as everyone on the bus sat in silence, listening to the violence of the storm. The wăng luò feed ceased. Occasional bits of debris slammed into the side of the bus. Then, the bus moved. It was a slight movement, but it had definitely moved.

"Oh my god!" Rosario said. "What now?"

"Everyone make sure you have a seat cushion," the director said. "We don't want to be trapped inside the bus if it is swept out to sea and then sinks. If this bus starts to drift, we may have to abandon it.

"Maybe not," Antonio said.

Antonio got everyone to empty their luggage. In all they had twenty one bags.

"We're going to fill these bags with sand and load them into the baggage compartment. The extra weight will keep our wheels on the ground a little longer."

"What about the coyotes?" Marisa asked.

"We'll take several people out. Some to work and some to stand guard. I'm confident coyotes won't attack a large, vigilant group."

Just about everyone stood up to help.

"No, wait!" Antonio said. "If we all get off the bus, it may float away right now. Just give me two people to work and two more to stand guard. Beto, you're one of my guards."

"I'm responsible for all this," Director Contreras said. "I will go."

Officer Clemente stood up. "Me, too."

"No, you're wounded and suffering from hypothermia. You can't go out," Antonio said.

"I'm good enough. Plus I'm an adult and I don't want any kids going out there that don't have to go. I've spent more time in the desert and in the surf chasing smugglers than anyone in here. I know how to handle myself."

Antonio reluctantly agreed.

"I'll be on guard with Beto," said Sister Elizondo, as she grabbed the fire extinguisher.

Once outside, the plan was for Clemente, Rosario, Antonio, and the director to fill all the luggage with sand and stash it in the luggage compartment at the bottom of the bus. Beto and Sister Elizondo would stand watch for coyotes. As soon as they stepped out of the bus, their feet sunk into the sand. The water was up to their knees. Just getting to the side of the bus to open the luggage compartment was a challenge. And visibility was so low, they had no idea if anything dangerous was nearby. Nevertheless, they began to work.

They had nothing but their hands to dig with, but the sand was soft. The waves swept into the cargo hold. And then Beto saw movement.

"Coyotes!" he yelled.

Antonio stood up and turned around. He could see the animals watching from a distance. Would they attack or would they keep their distance? No one moved. And then Antonio saw movement to his left. Beto had just launched a projectile. And then he slung another. And then another. Antonio couldn't tell if any of the projectiles hit their mark, but the coyotes began to back away.

Antonio and the others quickly began their work again. Sister Elizondo stood behind them with the fire extinguisher. And Beto kept slinging projectiles until the coyotes were out of sight. It didn't take long before all the bags were heavy from the wet sand inside them. They closed the luggage compartment and Antonio hoped it would be enough weight to make a difference.

By the time they were back on the bus and changed into dry clothes, another hour had passed. The storm was still strong but it didn't seem to be getting any worse. Everyone bunched together for warmth and tried to get some sleep. Antonio insisted on staying awake as a sentry to announce whatever bad news might come next. But nothing came. As the sky began to brighten with dawn, the bus was still in place.

The rest of the day was long and boring. All they could do was wait. The eye of the storm passed over them just after dawn. The wind and rain stopped. The sun shone for a brief moment, but then the storm returned. By late afternoon, the worst was over.

The group was hungry and thirsty. They collected what water they could from the rain, but it didn't seem to be enough. The rain continued into the night.

The next morning, the rain had become just a drizzle. The road was still flooded. Antonio asked for volunteers to attempt the ten mile hike to the school.

"There may be food and shelter there," he said.

In the end, they decided they would all go. It was a long, wet hike. The water in the low-water crossings came up to their waists or a little higher, but Antonio and Rosario knew how to move people safely across such obstacles.

At one point, Dr. Esquivel fell to her knees. "I don't know how much longer I can go on," she said. She wasn't just being dramatic. They were all dehydrated and exhausted. Whereas the cool weather had been a problem during the long, wet nights, heat was the problem now. The sun was beating down on them mercilessly.

Beto looked around and saw nothing that would offer shade. They had no choice but to keep walking. It couldn't be much further than a mile or so. Grace and Marisa helped Dr. Esquivel to her feet and they stumbled on. It took most of the day until they were close enough to see the school in the distance. It had survived the storm!

As they approached the school, Mr. Stewart walked out into the road to greet them. "Mr. Silva and I have the solar array working a little bit, so we have a little electricity. And the water tanks survived, so we have water."

Rosario and Marisa carried Dr. Esquivel into the reception area of the academic building. They sat her in a cushioned chair and got her some water. Everyone was sunburned and thirsty. They drank lots of water and Antonio raided the kitchen and brought back a case of NutriVitaPro breakfast discs. The students tore into them. The adults were less enthusiastic, but they ate them anyway.

"How did the buildings do?" the director asked.

"Could be worse," Mr. Stewart said. "Come and see."

Some second and third floor windows had been broken on the seaward side of the classroom building. The dorms were a little better off.

"We'll have some water damage to repair," Mr. Stewart said.

Just then, they turned the corner and saw the auditorium. The seaward side had collapsed.

"I think the old auditorium is gone," Mr. Stewart said. "It was a beautiful old theater."

Not only had the brick wall crumbled, but the floor and ceiling were sagging, having lost many of their supports. Underneath the auditorium floor, in the secret basement, nothing remained. The waves had washed away whatever was in the basement, including the old man's body. Beto was now the only one at the school who knew the old man had died there.

Chapter 25 - After the Apocalypse

In which the school reopens.

It took several weeks to get all the windows repaired. It took longer to rip out the water-damaged walls and rebuild them all. But most of the school was functional by the Christmas break. The director sent out notices to all the students' families that school would resume after the first of the year.

Beto and Marisa became experts at floating drywall and they now considered Mr. Silva somewhat of a friend. On December 17, a wrecking machine took down what remained of the auditorium.

It was a cold night as the remaining staff and students built a campfire on the beach to celebrate all the work they had done. Dr. Esquivel, who had returned to her university, came to join in the celebration. Officer Clemente had been invited, but had declined the invitation. They had seen little of her once the roads had reopened.

Marisa was watching for signs of romance between Dr. Esquivel and Director Contreras now that it was clear that there was love but no romance between the director and Maestra Solis. Honestly, she just couldn't tell. The director was so formal and brooding. He might never be able to let anyone into his life again.

Dr. Esquivel stood by the director and she raised her cup of hot chocolate.

"The first thing I would like to say, having survived a hurricane with you all, is please stop calling me Dr. Esquivel. My name is Celeste. Since we almost died together, the least you can do is address me by my first name. Until classes start again, at least. It will make me feel more human."

The group raised their cups and shouted their approval.

"Celeste," Marisa said to Beto. "It means 'the heavenly one,' in Latin. Very appropriate."

Director Contreras raised his cup as well.

"You may all refer to me as… Director Contreras. I am still your headmaster."

Everyone laughed.

Dr. Esquivel put an arm around the director's shoulders. "I'll call you Justo, even if no one else does."

"Can we rename the school now that we have rebuilt it?" Marisa said. "Why would you call an international school The Lindheimer Academy?"

"Actually, Ferdinand Lindheimer was an immigrant—a German immigrant," Dr. Esquivel said. "He discovered as much about the native life of this continent as perhaps any other individual. Maybe it is appropriate that this school, struggling with the big modern issue of making peace with the natural world, should be named after him."

"Yeah, but it's so... White," Marisa said. "And this school is so international...multicultural."

Mr. Stewart gave Marisa a friendly nudge. "Multicultural implies room for multiple cultures. Including white people, like me."

"Okay, we're very mixed. But Lindheimer sounds so European," Marisa said. "Can't we have a name more representative of who we are—African, Asian, la Raza...?"

Everyone looked at the director.

"I tell you what," he said. "When all the students return we can have that discussion."

Everyone voiced their agreement.

"And then I'll discuss it with the Board of Directors and the donor who gave the money to purchase the school, and who requested that it be named after Lindheimer."

Everyone moaned.

"We'll see," the director said. "We survived being stranded in a hurricane. Anything is possible."

"Tell us, Celeste," Antonio said. "Even though your research was interrupted by the hurricane, are there any results you can share with us about our school's mythos?"

Dr. Esquivel nodded and seemed thoughtful for a moment.

"I still have much work to do. And the storm has interfered greatly. But it has also been an interesting event in the sense that I've been able to observe the students and staff in an intense time period."

"Yeah," Marisa said. "We survived an apocalypse."

"That's a great word choice," Dr. Esquivel said. "So

often, people use the word apocalypse as if it means the end of the world or the end of time."

"I was just using hyperbole," Marisa said, looking slightly unsure of herself. "It doesn't mean the end of the world?"

"Not at all. It simply means a time when something is revealed or uncovered, usually something very important. Calypso, the name of the goddess, means to hide, just like she hid Odysseus for several years. *Apo-calypse* means to unhide or to reveal."

"So the apocalypse in the Bible…?" Beto asked

"It's the revelation of the kingdom of God, which has been here all along, but hidden," Dr. Esquivel said.

"Interesting," Beto said.

"And so this storm is our apocalypse because…?" Marisa asked.

"Seeing you all work together to rebuild your school has revealed something about you. Before, your director talked a lot about self-sufficiency, but now, I've seen physical evidence of it. Students with wrecking tools in their hands tearing out old walls, and then rebuilding them… That will be a part of your story forever."

It was January 8. The parking lot was full of parents unloading their children's luggage. Several Border Patrol vehicles were present, as usual.

Beto and Gonzalo, who had returned to school just that morning, watched from the second floor as vehicles carrying students arrived.

"Did you tell anybody about the body?" Gonzalo

asked.

"No," Beto said. "Since I hadn't seen it, I didn't really know what to say. But I did ask Mr. Silva about the basement and he said that migrants were always trying to get into it, to use it as a safe refuge. No one from the school ever went down there. He said he thought it wasn't safe."

"Why wasn't it safe?"

"The Navy had stored some nasty chemicals down there. He did his best to seal all the outside doors, but he said people still found a way in on occasion. So maybe the old man was just looking for a safe place and just happened to die while he was there."

"Sad," Gonzalo said. "I guess we'll never find out."

The two boys continued to watch out the window for their friends.

A very new, very shiny, big black electrosedan pulled into the parking lot. Officer Clemente was the first person to approach the vehicle. She examined the papers handed to her and then handed them back. A man stepped out of the car and began to pull luggage from the trunk. Adriana stepped out from the passenger side.

Beto ran down the stairs to meet her. He ran across the parking lot, waved to Officer Clemente, and then gave Adriana a kiss on the cheek.

"It's good to see you," Beto said.

Adriana smiled. "Beto, I'd like you to meet my father. Papa, this is my friend, Beto."

"It's an honor to meet you, sir," Beto said.

"Mucho gusto," Señor Cavazos Aguilar replied.

Beto helped carry Adriana's luggage in. He gave her some space as she said good-bye to her father. Her father waved at Beto as he left, and then gave Beto the "I'm watching you" sign, pointing two fingers first to his own eyes and then pointing at Beto. But he smiled as he did this.

"Your dad seems nice," Beto said.

"He's a good dad," Adriana said.

Beto stood at the door as Adriana began to unpack her things.

"I guess I should tell you that Officer Clemente said some stuff about your dad."

"Stuff?" Adriana replied. "You've been spending time with Officer Clemente?"

"We were stuck on the same bus for two days during the hurricane."

"Listen. I can guess what she said. And yes, it's true. My family has cartel connections. I guess I should have told you sooner."

"Oh, wow," Beto said. "I didn't necessarily believe Clemente. She's pretty paranoid."

"But no, it's true," Adriana said. "That's my life. I can afford to come to a good school in a safe place, while a lot of my childhood friends aren't as lucky. Do you hate me now? 'Cause sometimes I hate myself for all the privileges I have."

Adriana's eyes began to fill with tears. Her real eye turned red, the other stayed pretty much the same. Impulsively, Beto stepped forward and pulled her into a hug.

"I don't hate you," he said. "I don't think I could

ever hate you. But that's a big part of your life I guess I'm going to have to learn about. It's a part of who you are."

"It really isn't," Adriana said. "I want to be as far from that life as I can. And my dad agrees. But I'll always be conected to it. I'll never be competely safe. And no one I care about will ever be completely safe."

"We have the rest of the school year to learn about each other," Beto said. "I've got a ton of stories from surviving the hurricane."

"But listen. I don't want you to think I hate my dad. And I don't want you to think he's a bad person. He's a businessman, doing the only kind of business possible for him. Between corrupt government and corrupt businesses, he just does what he has to to provide for his family."

Beto let this sink in for a few moments.

"I just want to be your friend," Beto said, still holding Adriana close. "And I know you have a good heart. Everything else can wait."

Chapter 26 - The End and the Beginning

In which the plan of Director Contreras takes a step forward.

The two women sat by the little fire as the sun went down. The older woman was about to put the fire out, when the younger woman stopped her.

"Catalina, stop," she said. The younger woman pointed out into the desert. "They are coming."

A small family was approaching the camp—a man, a woman, and two young children. They were being led by Antonio and Rosario. Grace walked in the rear and escorted the children.

"We have our first family," Antonio said. "They were on the verge of being deported. Their home village is too dangerous to return to. And they have experience living in the desert from when they first crossed the border."

Acknowledgments

Thanks to the creative minds behind Story Sanctum and all the great stories they are bringing into the world. Special thanks to the thoughtful and detailed editing of Shawn Casselberry. Shawn has improved this book in countless ways and all remaining imperfections are my responsibility.

Thanks to the students, parents, faculty and staff of the Presbyterian Pan American School for welcoming me into your community. I am still amazed at the courage of high school students who are willing to leave home, travel to a new country, and study in a new culture while learning a new language. You guys are my heroes.

Finally, thanks to my wife, Sonja, for the time and space for me to disappear for countless hours in order to write these stories.

About the Author

Doug Dalglish has always wanted to travel everywhere and do everything. He has been a US Marine, an electrical engineer, and a Presbyterian minister. He has also been active in the Texas Master Naturalist program for more than twenty years, studying the intricate details of the natural world. For seven years, he was the head of staff of a residential high school, located in a remote and isolated location. He and his wife, Sonja, live on the Guadalupe River, about 170 miles east of Ciudad Acuña, Mexico, and have four adult children.

www.ingramcontent.com/pod-product-compliance
Lightning Source LLC
Chambersburg PA
CBHW022150170626
46807CB00005B/2147